Also by Carl Dane:
Hawke and Carmody Western Novels
Valley of the Lesser Evil
Canyon of the Long Shadows
Rage under the Red Sky

Rapid Fire Reads (short books)
Delta of the Dying Souls
The Mountain of Slow Madness
Fury on the Far Horizon

THE ADVENTURES OF HAWKE AND CARMODY

CARL DANE

RAGING BULL PUBLISHING

Dedication

To Mark and Carl III

Introduction

Thanks for picking up this collection of short stories. They are some of the works I had the most fun writing and I hope you'll find the same enjoyment reading them.

Excessively kind reviewers of my work have noted that they become engrossed in the interplay of the diverse characters whose lives have intertwined in that turbulent time I suppose you'd call the "Early Wild West" – the decade or so after the Civil War. It was a time when men and women who had been forever changed by extraordinary upheaval were trying to regain their balance, figure out where they were heading, and in the process figure out who they really were.

For those of you new to this series, Josiah Hawke was a young college professor before the war and found that his true skills lay in battles, not books. Tom Carmody had been a Tennessee mountain man who grew up, as Hawke characterized it, "eating squirrels in hills so strange and remote that even non-native squirrels shunned the place." Carmody's knowledge of the land turned him into a legendary scout and tracker for the Union Army. The beautiful Elmira Adler had been kidnapped as a child by the Apaches but escaped, and with her late husband founded a reasonably successful bar and bordello in Texas Hill Country.

All three were brought into each other's orbit when the marshal in Elmira's town was murdered. He'd left word with Elmira to summon Hawke – who had been a lieutenant under the murdered marshal's command in an elite Union special-tactics outfit – in the event of just such an occurrence. Hawke agreed to take the late marshal's job, deputized Carmody – who he'd found languishing in the town jail after single-handedly beating up a dozen men who'd tried to cheat him at cards – and unraveled a complex mystery that involved greed, corruption, and an unspeakable secret.

In this collection, we see the trio – who share great respect and affection for each other but nonetheless occasionally grate on each other's nerves – facing unique problems. In *Delta,* Hawke ponders an ethical dilemma about what to do with a terminally ill gunfighter who wants to goad Hawke into killing him. In *Mountain,* Carmody is captured by a violent cult and must employ his considerable gift for blarney (which Hawke occasionally characterizes with a less-elegant word) to outwit his captors. And in *Fury,* Hawke confronts a woman from his past, a Confederate spy who had tried to kill him and is now in the company of a war criminal who Hawke was once dispatched to kill.

Enjoy! And please visit my website, www.carldane.com, and find out more about past and upcoming books in the series.

With Respect, Dear Reader –

Carl Dane

DELTA

OF THE DYING

SOULS

A HAWKE & CARMODY
WESTERN SHORT STORY

CARL DANE

RAGING BULL PUBLISHING

The only way I can explain what happened is that a bullet has to go *somewhere*.

Sometimes projectiles find their target in a man's chest or head, or cut off an ear lobe, or fly wild, winding up in a ceiling, wall, or floorboard. And then there are the cases men endlessly recount in the saloons — freak occurrences when the round was deflected by a belt buckle or buried harmlessly in a Bible in someone's breast pocket.

My point – and trust me, I do have one – is that if you shoot at a man who is 70 inches tall by 30 inches wide, that's 2,100 square inches, and as the bullet has to go *somewhere,* there are roughly the same odds of it hitting a square inch in his chest, the belt, or his breast pocket.

Or, in my case, as hitting the barrel of his revolver and tearing it out of his grip.

Had I not dawdled in drawing on Jake Spencer I probably would have killed him with a clean shot to the heart. And had he not dithered in drawing on me, for reasons I could not explain, either, I would have been dead.

And had none of this happened, I wouldn't have wound up in the papers as the lawman who took mercy on a legendary but aging gunfighter and shot the gun out of his hand.

Let me back up and tell you the story from the beginning. My name is Josiah Hawke, and I'm the marshal in a sad little town called

Shadow Valley in the Hill Country of Texas. I came here a while ago to find the killer of the previous marshal, a fellow named Billy Gannon, who had been the captain of my unit in the war. Gannon had left word to contact me if anything happened to him, and something did – he took four bullets to the side of his head.

I found who killed Gannon and killed him, and then inertia took over. This woebegone little hamlet, so out-of-the-way that it couldn't even find an undertaker after the old one died – leaving me stuck with the duty of burying anybody I shoot — feels like home to me now. I have a sometime girlfriend, a woman named Elmira who owns a local bar and bordello, and a deputy named Carmody who is from eastern Tennessee and spouts downhome wisdom nonstop and sometimes makes me wonder about the wisdom of my carrying a gun when I'm around him.

But my exasperation is tempered by the fact that Carmody has saved my life more than I've saved his. I keep count.

Anyway, the story began when Jake Spencer got the drop on me as I turned a corner near my office.

"Hawke, this is for killing my son," he said, and without further discussion went for his gun.

I hadn't seen Jake Spencer in eight years, not since we did some lawing together in New

Mexico. I almost didn't recognize him; his hair and mustache had gone a yellowish white and he was much thinner than I remembered.

I certainly didn't expect to see Spencer nor did I expect him to pull on me, not over something that happened almost a decade ago.

Yes, I'd killed his son, a wild-eyed, slack-jawed idiot, then in his mid-30s, who'd gotten drunk and started shooting up a bar with me in it – and who would have thoroughly ventilated me and some other bystanders had I not returned fire.

And yes, the incident was made far more troubling by the fact that Jake Spencer had saved my life not much than a month before I killed his boy. I'd been pinned down, alone, by four rustlers. I'd forgotten to pack enough brains and ammunition that day, and would have been shot all to hell had not Spencer ridden down on the rustlers, fully exposed on a downslope with no cover, firing his revolver while his horse galloped at full speed. Spencer survived with a graze to his leg. All the rustlers wound up feeding the worms; he picked off three, and I killed the fourth with my last bullet.

Well, nobody ever promised me that life wouldn't be complicated.

Spencer was crushed by the grief any father would feel after the incident in the bar. I'd gone to the funeral, as uncomfortable an hour as I'd ever experienced. After we'd thrown dirt on the coffin, he had solemnly told me that as a fellow lawman he realized that I had no choice but to do what I did.

I believed him and we shook hands.

With that, we'd parted ways, until now, until this strange moment when he appeared out of nowhere and drew on me.

I hesitated, a habit that will get you dead, but in the split-second I had to make a decision I recognized him despite the years and the change in his countenance. I'm unusually good with names and faces, a handy skill in my line of work. It took me a second to react because I was derailed by the image of the Jake Spencer extending a hand and not the business end of a revolver.

Spencer hesitated, too. It wasn't much, just a hitch as the tip of the barrel cleared the polished back leather of his holster, maybe the physical manifestation of a second thought. It gave me time to clear the holster but not to aim.

Most of the time a panic-shot goes into the ceiling or the shooter's foot. Mine happened to find the one-square-inch tip of his barrel as he leveled out his weapon.

The gun, a big Colt, spun crazily past his shoulder and landed a good ten feet behind him.

Spencer looked at his empty hand, flexed it and found it uninjured, and looked at me as though I'd just pulled off the world's most amazing magic trick.

Which I guess I did, although by accident.

"The *fuck?*" he said, looking back down at his palm.

I was going to explain my theory about the 2,100 square inches, but instead I just clubbed him over the head with my gun barrel and dragged him to the jail.

At about noon the next day, Tom Carmody sat on the bench in front of my office and stamped his feet with delight as he read the front page of the *Dead Horse Hill Gazette*, published in a town 30 miles west of us, a comparative metropolis. The paper had been dropped off by the driver of the afternoon stage.

"Well, *shit!*" he said in his mountain twang. It came out, *wahl shee-it.*

"Says here you 'cemented your reputation as the lawman with the lightning draw by shooting the gun out of the hand of legendary gunfighter Jake Spencer.'"

I said nothing. I didn't want to encourage him.

"Gives a roundup of a few of the set-tos you've had in town since you came here and started filling up your own wing of our pitiful little cemetery," Camody continued.

He stamped his feet again. "Haha! Lookie here...says you is also known for your 'furious fists.'"

He stabbed a finger at the page. "I kid you not. Says right here. Maybe someday somebody'll write a book about you, 'Josiah Hawke, the Fists of Fury.'"

Carmody folded the paper and leaned back on the bench. He rubbed his wiry black beard and regarded me thoughtfully.

"Never knew no 'lawman with the lightning draw' before," he said. "I am deeply grateful to you for filling that void. But a few things I don't get here. Says Jake Spencer was a gunfighter. You told me he was a lawman. Guess he worked both sides of the street?"

"Yeah, like a lot of men I ran with after the war," I said. "But as far as I know, his gunwork was mostly guarding stagecoaches, fighting off rustlers, keeping the peace in gambling houses, stuff like that, usually a pace or two on the right side of the law, though sometimes we'd straddle the line. We were both deputized in '70 to handle a range war. We both drifted in and out of lawing since then."

"But the thing about his son?"

I didn't respond right away because I didn't actually have a good answer and wanted to think for a minute. I leaned on the fire barrel next to the bench and contemplated the scenery along Front Street.

Towns like Shadow Valley are mostly old slapdash wood buildings, a lot of them connected and more than a few sharing a common attic, which I've been told allows the rapid spread of flames. Fires in places like this are an ominous and ever-present threat, hence the water barrels in front of every fourth building or so. From my perspective, the barrel on the boardwalk outside my office also provides good cover. It's taken two bullets for me so far. Saved my life almost as often as Carmody.

Tom Carmody hailed from the mountains of Eastern Tennessee. He'd served the Union with the Tennessee Volunteer Infantry, mostly as a scout and tracker. He could read terrain like you or I read a newspaper.

Carmody was tall, about six-five, and had one of those deceptively powerful backwoods builds: Long limbs, ropey veins in thin arms, broad shoulders, and huge hands.

Even though lately he'd taken to wearing polished boots, a leather vest, and a neatly blocked derby, he somehow still gave the impression that he'd just stepped out of a cabin in the woods. Somehow, the man could make a three-piece suit look like stained buckskins and a straw hat.

"I don't know what that's about," I said, finally. "Spencer won't talk to me much – he just lies in the cell most of the time. He said it's been eating at him all these years that I shot his son and that was it."

"And you don't buy what he said?"

"No. Not entirely. Of course I can understand him being angry about his son, but why *now* and not *then?*"

"And you had no choice," Carmody said.

"None. He was firing wild into a room full of people."

"So you had no choice but to let loose with the lightning draw. If he was shooting, there wasn't no way to whale away with them furious fists of yours."

I let it pass.

I made it a point to swing by the bank and the Silver Spoon on my rounds later that day.

The bank was located at the end of town where Front Street took an erratic diagonal turn to avoid a flat, marshy area in back, where two small rivers had created a wide delta that deposited a bleak, flat floor of gray sediment for as far as you could see in back. I was told that the bank was one of the oldest buildings in town, probably built with the presumption that it would be the center of town, which is the case with most banks. But the town grew with a mind of its own, and entrepreneurs who put up new buildings quite sensibly did so several hundred yards away on higher, drier land.

I was doing double rounds near the bank because there was a load of silver there, deposited by one stagecoach to await pickup by another that would continue the transport route to Austin.

Only Carmody, I, and the agent from the stagecoach company knew about the silver, the agent had told me.

I wasn't particularly worried. Bank robberies aren't as common as you might suspect from reading dime novels. Valuables are a hell of a lot easier to steal from a stage or train than from a building with a safe and reinforced doors.

Still, a load of silver — valued, I was told, at about ten thousand dollars — is a powerful moron magnet. I knew that anything could happen.

Elmira was in a better mood when I stepped into the Silver Spoon, her combination bar, casino, and bordello. The day had gotten off to a rocky start when we woke up in her room above the bar and – as usual — she got up late and couldn't find the clothes she planned to wear that day.

A slow learner, I'd innocently pointed out to her that we had hung around in her room pretty much the entire night before doing absolutely nothing in particular, and I wondered why she hadn't looked for her clothes then.

She icily informed me that last night she didn't know that she wouldn't be able to find them in the morning.

You can't argue with logic like that, so I didn't try.

I ordered a whiskey, and, as I have gotten in the habit of doing, sat down and played the upright piano for a few minutes.

I'd studied music. In fact, I'd studied a lot of things: Greek, Latin, philosophy, history, and science. I'd been a professor before the war, and had been trained as sort of a guerilla fighter when I enlisted in '61, and found out I was a quick study in the ways of killing we had been taught, and in fact was a much better fighter than a professor.

When my unit was disbanded in '65 I'd tried a halfhearted return to teaching, and it lasted a month. A prizefighter in a traveling carnival that had come to town goaded me into the ring, in full view of a gaggle of friends and students, and bet me big odds that I couldn't last two rounds with him.

Guess I didn't look like much of a threat to him. I'm not much over six feet tall and while I have wide shoulders and big hands I'm on the lean side, and even then, when I was in my early 30s, my hair and mustache had started to show some gray.

But I'd learned a lot in my raider unit, and I began to pick him apart without much effort. In a rage he tried to gouge out my eye, to which I did not take kindly, and I responded by methodically beating him to death.

And then I left my hometown and my career, one step ahead of a deputy sheriff.

I spent a few years as a bareknuckle fighter and drifted into the life of an itinerant lawman, winding up in Shadow Valley — the ass end of nowhere but a place not without its charms, one of which was Elmira Adler.

She was an innocent who had been swept up in the storm of violence that claimed the life of Marshal Gannon and ultimately forced me to kill about a dozen people. I'd saved her business, and that entitles me, among other prerogatives, to free drinks and exclusive access to the upright piano. I play in the bar most nights.

Elmira, her earlier bad mood a thing of the past, sat down beside me on the bench and smiled. She had golden hair with a few strands of silver and while there were what are politely called "laugh lines" around her eyes, her face showed none of the ravages of the hard life of prostitution that are often clawed into the visages of the women we call, with equal politeness, "doves."

Elmira Alder had gone into business with her late husband and moved into management, so to speak, and treated her girls well and showed compassion for the down-and-outers who pass through these parts. If they needed a meal, she'd provide one. Should they need their head bandaged up after they'd gotten drunk and started trouble and I'd whacked them with the barrel of my Colt, Elmira would take care of that, too.

She looked so chipper that for a second I was afraid she was going to sing. She is truly tone-deaf, which I happen to know is actually a rare condition. Almost all people can approximate a pitch, and the fact that they can't hit the note precisely is only apparent to them because they have the ability to distinguish that they are off-key. Elmira had no such faculty nor inhibitions, and was wont to let loose with sounds like what you'd expect from wounded wildlife.

She didn't sing. She wanted to talk about the newspaper article.

I wished she would have broken into song.

"You shot the gun out of that man's hand yesterday at about noon, and it wound up the Dead Horse Hill paper this morning. Amazing that the news of your trick shot traveled that fast."

I played a little louder.

"The telegraph operator," I said. "He freelances. Sends some stuff to editors, they take the bare bones and flesh them out with any old phony stuff they think will sell papers, and thus legends are born."

"You *are* a legend," she said, as tone-deaf to sarcasm as she was to musical pitch. "He was a famous gunfighter, but he must be what – 70? – and you took pity on him and shot the gun out of his hand."

I hit the next chord harder than necessary.

"I did *not* shoot the gun out of his hand. I mean, I *did*, technically, but it was a wild shot, a one-in-a-million thing. I recognized Spencer and actually thought he was going to say hello to me. I froze when he drew and by the time I reacted all I could do was pull and fire in his direction. I just as easily could have shot myself in the leg. Now I wish I had."

"Maybe you should wire the paper and ask for a correction."

I said nothing.

"Although I suppose it doesn't hurt for someone in your line of work to be feared. I mean, if I were a robber in this town I would never mess with the 'lawman with the lightning draw.' And it's been pretty peaceful in here today, even though it's payday for the cattle drive – probably because no one wants to get your big fist of fury to their jaw."

I switched to *Green Grow the Lilacs*, a spirited Irish ballad we sung during the war. You can play it nice and loud and it has a steady three-quarter beat with no quiet parts. Useful under the circumstances.

"Anyway, I just wanted to catch up on the day," she said, in that tone that generally serves as an overture to a stream of random and disconnected thoughts.

"I found my dress. It was under the bed. Anything else interesting? Oh, I heard there's ten thousand dollars in silver at the bank."

"Fucking *hell.*" I was standing, the piano was ringing softly with the echo of the last chord I'd pounded out, and every eye in the place was turned on me.

"Josiah, *sit down.*"

"Sorry," I said, and sat back and the bench. I started playing and stared straight ahead while I talked to her through clenched teeth.

"Who told you that? For God's sake, if anybody finds out that much silver is in that rickety old bank we could have big trouble."

She looked at me with those cheerful blue eyes, wide as half-dollars and blue as a mountain lake, and chirped: "Oh, I don't remember exactly who. I mean, everybody knows..."

I stopped playing and she put a hand on my shoulder.

"*Please* don't go jumping around crazy again."

Carmody and I worked out a schedule where one of us would be at the bank right through until tomorrow morning when the stage would arrive to pick up the silver. Stage-coaches carrying cash or precious metals were generally well-protected, and once the stage and its cargo left the town limits they were no longer my problem.

The stagecoach agent who'd warned me about the "secret" deposit was no longer in town, but in any event, I wouldn't be able to pin the leak on him. Even if I did there's no law against talking too much and too stupid. If there were, we'd have to build a jail on every block.

And I had no proof it was the agent I'd spoken too. There's a chain of people involved in any supposed "secret" – clerks, telegraph operators, drivers, and the like – and once gossip gets out in a town where the residents have two saloons and a lot of time on their hands word is going to spread.

Carmody took the first watch.

I had some business to settle with Jake Spencer.

He was stretched out on the cot and didn't make much noise except to cough a lot. He was thinner than I remembered, his coal-black hair and mustache had withered to a thin straw, and his eyes had lost a lot of their light. But you could still see the whipcord in his build beneath the baggy suit. He looked like he could still take care of himself, after a fashion, but no longer cared enough to try.

"You've been playing clam for 24 hours," I said. "Maybe if we can get to the bottom of this you can get out of this cell. But I can't let you loose until I'm sure you're not going to plug me or somebody else. So, I'll ask one more time. You can talk straight with me or pee in that bucket until the outhouse trip tomorrow morning."

"A fair chance, that's all I ask," Spencer said, and then he coughed into a handkerchief. "In the street. You can handle it. You and your lightning draw."

Obviously, Carmody had talked to him earlier.

"Jake, *why?* I thought we'd settled this years ago."

"*You owe me!*"

It was a scream, and it had suddenly come from somewhere deeper than deep, a private hell in the depths of his soul. I was startled. Shaken.

"I owe you my life," I said, after giving myself a second to calm down. "I'm not disputing that. But what does that have to do with you wanting to kill me? My God, what the hell is going on?"

He turned to face me. His eyes were gray where they should have been white and were rimmed all round by red.

"A chance to make everything square. That's all I ask."

I didn't know what to add so I left.

It was raining.

The bank closed in an hour and I was due to take the watch from Carmody at seven or thereabouts. The time was sort of collective hunch in Shadow Valley because only a few people had timepieces and the bank clock, which served as our master clock, was set on a what was essentially a guess by the manager, who once a week or so looked skyward and proclaimed that it was noon.

There was a railroad coming soon and we'd probably have to get a little more organized, but for now, close enough was close enough.

If I were free, I'd sometimes stop at the Spoon at four, or what I thought was four, to take the afternoon receipts to the bank. But sometimes Elmira made the trip, as apparently she was planning on doing today. I walked in at the same time she was leaving.

She was carrying an umbrella, a cloth deposit bag, and a straw basket.

"Dinner for Tom," she said. "You've kept the poor man at the bank all day."

"I'll take it," I said. "It's raining."

"I'm not made of sugar," she said, and unfurled the umbrella. I noted that the contents of the basket made a telltale clanking noise of bot-

tle-on-bottle. That would be Carmody's idea of
a two-course dinner.

I let her run the errand. I needed a drink
and a few minutes to think. My lightning draw
was not necessary to protect the modest afternoon receipts, in any event. As backward and as
occasionally violent as Shadow Valley was, it
was in typical of the towns I'd seen throughout
the West. A woman on the street was given a
wide berth, and if a man jostled or accosted her
there would generally be hell to pay from
passersby. Such gallantry was not the norm in
most places in my native Illinois nor in most of
the Eastern cities in which I'd traveled. Of
course, back East it was also significantly less
likely you'd be gunned down over a card game,
so I guess things even out.

I sat at a corner table and made myself
look as uncompanionable as possible. I needed
to think and didn't want conversation, especially about that newspaper article, and my expression let everyone know that they were risk-
ing a furious fucking fist if they intruded.

On my mind was what to do about
Spencer. I had a hunch about what was going
on and it made me more depressed than before.
There was no way I could verify my suspicion at
that moment. Shadow Valley didn't have a full-
time doctor and I'm not sure that the old man
with the thick glasses who came by every few
days to patch up broken bones and the like had

actually ever seen the inside of a classroom anyway. In fact, I'd heard rumors that he worked on horses, too, but I can't verify that.

I was no closer to a solution but the whiskey had mellowed my mood a little by the time I heard the first gunshots.

It took me about fifteen seconds to run down Front Street and locate the source of the volleys.

Carmody was firing from the roof of the bank. Like a mountain goat, he always preferred the view from high terrain and had stationed himself there while on watch. Six men on horseback were firing up at him, and two riderless horses were hitched outside. While it could be the case two people from out of town had ridden in for an appointment at the bank, I assumed there were two robbers within.

There was a laundry and a barber shop at the bend before the road turned to the left to avoid the marshy delta in back of the bank. I took cover behind the laundry, which was on my right, and fired left-handed so as not to expose myself. Even though I'm right-handed, I've practiced so I can shoot just as well with my left, one of those skills impressed on us in my training.

The robbers scattered behind the left side of the bank building and began to poke around the corner and sporadically return fire. Their attention was now directed in two directions – me and the roof – but there were six of them and two of us and for the time being it was a standoff.

But as things stood, we were destined to be on the losing end of this game. Carmody and I were outgunned and the actions of the men presumably inside the bank amounted to a wild card.

Only two men in town could be counted on to help Carmody and me. One was the black-smith, a sturdy young man named Richard Oak, and the other the sour-faced druggist, Vern Miller. Oak had seen limited action in the Union Army and while I'd like to have him and his outsized shoulders on my side in a barroom brawl, I'd surmised during previous conversations that he knew little about guns.

Miller the druggist was a mystery; of his background he would speak not a syllable, but he had a habit of showing up in times of tension and looking as though he wouldn't mind a little dust-up.

I reflected on the fact that I'd never gotten around to putting together a vigilance committee or a group that I could deputize or collect into a posse. Most of the men at any given day in Shadow Valley were drifters, or part-time residents who would disappear and reappear with the wind and the cattle drives. Other men in town were too old, or too young, or too likely to shoot me in the back either by accident or on purpose.

"*Bank robbery!*" It was Oak, who had sidled up at my right elbow and scared the hell out of me. In addition to his grasp of the obvious, he possessed, I noted, a .22 rifle that from the looks of it may or may not have been fired in years, and appeared to have enough stopping power to lay out a squirrel, if the squirrel were on the dainty side.

"*Hold your fire!*" That was Carmody. He was looking down on the front door of the bank, which was open halfway. The door opened out and from my direction I couldn't see who or what was behind it. Carmody could.

Everyone immediately stopped shooting. Carmody had a very authoritative voice, and I wondered if would be worth a try to have him just scream at everybody to go home. Probably not.

Then the door opened all the way and two people stepped out. The one in back was a tall man with a mean face; he had a tight grip on the one in front and pressed a pistol pressed against her temple.

It was Elmira.

So we now had another standoff, and to make things more complicated the skies opened up and it began to pour. We had to shout to be heard over the rain and thunder. Best I could figure out, the guy holding the gun on Elmira wanted me and Carmody to back off and let them take the silver. They would release Elmira later, once they surmised that they were not being followed.

There were a couple of things I could deduce from what he said. One, he made no mention of the bank manager, who was usually the only employee inside late in the afternoon. That almost certainly meant he was dead. Two, they thought I was as moronic as they were, because they expected me to believe they would release a witness who could identify them as bank robbers and murderers.

Stupid, desperate people are dangerous, and something had to be done, and quickly.

I turned to Oak. He looked hypnotized. I backhanded him on the shoulder to snap him back to consciousness and told him to go to the jail, use the big key on the ring hanging above my desk, let Spencer out, and tell Spencer that he was going to get his chance to make things square.

I also told Oak to follow behind Spencer with every gun and round of ammunition he could carry from my office.

I said nothing and did not show myself in the three or four minutes it took for Spencer to arrive. It was better to let these peckerwoods stew for a while than to engage them in conversation, say the wrong thing, and start the action sooner than I wanted.

It was apparent that I wasn't dealing with master criminals. Lawmen rarely do. By and large the general public and the press that informs them have an overly charitable view of your average gang, which is a collection of losers and down-and-outers who multiply their stupidity as their numbers increase.

Last month a noted gang in Kansas – which had been portrayed in the papers as a band of noble, wily Robin Hoods – botched a safe-cracking when they realized no one had remembered the dynamite. They quarreled about whose fault it was and wound up shooting at each other.

Now, that's what makes your average gaggle of criminals so damned dangerous. They're unpredictable, scared, and stupid. It's a tough choice whether I'd rather face a competent killer who acts out of reason, no matter how twisted, or a group of skittish cowboys with little minds and big ideas.

And as Jake Spencer walked into view from behind the laundry, I reflected on the fact that I'd soon be dealing with both.

Spencer had taken the liberty of liberating a Dragoon revolver from the office to replace the one I'd ruined by shooting into the mouth of the barrel. He was welcome to the damned thing. It had belonged to Billy Gannon, the previous marshal, and by my estimation it was a clumsy weapon, way too heavy in the barrel, although I have to admit it made an excellent club. The Dragoon was so big that it didn't fit all the way into Spencer's holster.

"You wanted to go out with a bang," I said, raising my voice over the roaring rain, which already had turned the street to sucking mud. "Here's your chance."

He said nothing and betrayed no reaction.

I unpinned my town marshal's badge and stuck it on his vest.

"You've been deputized."

He nodded.

No one had moved, as far as I could see. Carmody remained perched above the door, the goon with the gun at Elmira's temple stood still as a statue and Elmira stood transfixed. I couldn't tell how scared she was because the rain had washed her hair completely over her face. Unless you looked close, you couldn't tell whether she was facing front or back.

What was going on behind the bank building, the back and the side I couldn't see, I had no way of knowing.

It was time to roll the dice.

"Here's the deal," I shouted. "You can take the silver and a hostage. It's not our silver, and not our fight."

The man with the gun to Elmira's head nodded, tentatively.

"But it only works on this condition: You let the girl go. She's *my* girl, and I'm not going to let you animals have your way with her on the trail."

The gunman's expression was a study in slow realization. The hard planes in his face shifted from surprise to puzzlement to anger. That worried me because Elmira was maybe a one-pound trigger pull away from death; I noted that the hammer on his gun was cocked.

Carmody could do nothing from his perch. Even if he drilled a perfect shot from above that somehow killed the gunman and missed Elmira, his dying reflex would set off the gun and blow her brains out.

"We won't dirty your precious little girl," he said. "Besides, you ain't got no choice in the matter," he said.

"I don't believe you, and you *do* have a choice. I'm going to make you a trade. A deputy for my girl. You'll have some real leverage with a deputy for a hostage. The hostage you've got now won't mean anything to anybody besides me. She's just a bar-girl."

Elmira stiffened and even though I couldn't see her face I could tell she was ready to say something but she felt the tip of the barrel against her skull and kept it to herself.

"All that buys me is more trouble," he said. "The law's going to look out for one if its own. We'll be marked men for life if we take a deputy."

"I'm not denying there's some truth in what you say. The law will be more interested in finding the kidnappers of a deputy than a bar-girl. But they'll also be more concerned about keeping the hostage alive. I'm trading you a blue chip for a white chip."

He looked like he was processing what I saw saying and I hurried to close the deal.

"And do you really think the law in these parts is going to go on an endless crusade to find a deputy from this rathole? You get a better deal my way. And anyway, it's also the only deal you've got."

He looked like he was going to speak but hesitated.

"And to tell you the truth," I said, "rather than see my girl used by you I'd kill her myself. I'll shoot her right now if you don't go along."

I could see Elmira's mouth moving under the flat helmet of wet hair that covered her face. The mask of hair was sucked in and then pushed out where he mouth would be. I couldn't hear what she was saying and had a feeling I didn't want to.

"Let me see him," the gunman said. "Have him walk out right in front of me, hands in the air. No guns. I see a gun and she dies and then he dies."

Spencer handed me the Dragoon.

"Keep it dry," he said. "These things misfire when water gets in the back. But otherwise it ain't a bad gun. Packs a hell of a wallop."

I nodded and marveled at how this situation had suddenly become another day at the office for us.

"You always carried a pocket pistol," Spencer said. "If it's not too big I'm going to hide it in my crotch."

In cooler months when I wore a jacket I carried a Cooper pocket five-shot, which is about five inches long. When it was too warm for a coat I kept a .41 Remington Saw Handle in my pants pocket or boot. The gun was only about three inches long and only held one round but it did have some stopping power. It was better than nothing.

Spencer fiddled around with it until he was satisfied it was nestled in a part of his nether regions where no cowboy would search. Without another word he marched toward the front door of the bank, his heels sucking in the deepening mud.

Spencer knew that time was critical and every second the gang had to think was one tick closer to the deal falling through.

When Spencer was ten feet in front of him, the gunman held up the flat of his hand.

"Now you behind the laundry, and you on the roof, throw your guns in front of me."

Carmody tossed down a pistol and a long gun. He wanted the surrender to look genuine, so he gave up both. But I'd bet even money he was holding another weapon. He was so long and rangy you could stuff some light artillery under his jacket and no one would notice.

I was going to toss out the Dragoon and my personal sidearm but the blacksmith tapped me on the shoulder, scaring the crap out of me again. For a fellow his size he sure crept around like a cat. I'd keep that in mind as he might prove useful to me someday, as long as I didn't wind up shooting him by mistake.

Oak had brought back a pile of guns. I picked up a couple of junky single-actions and tossed them around the corner. And I threw the Dragoon out there, too.

When it happened, the exchange was over in a second. The gunman shoved Elmira forward, but as her feet were sunk ankle-deep in the mud she couldn't take a quick forward step and she fell face-forward flat in the soup. The gunman kept his pistol trained on Elmira and motioned to a man inside who warily came out front, pistol in hand, and grabbed the reins of the two horses and led them out of sight to where the rest of the gang had presumably nested.

The gunman then grabbed Spencer by the collar, pointed the gun at his head, and quickly steered him through the door.

I rushed over to Elmira and pried her loose. There was a slurping sound when her body emerged from the mud.

No point it trying to prod her to run: I carried her back to cover at the side of the laundry and interrogated her as quickly as I could. It was an odd experience as I actually couldn't tell her front from her back what with the hair and the mud and she kept coughing and spitting but I managed to find out what I needed to know in a desperate hurry.

The bank manager was dead. They'd made him open the safe and shot him when they thought he was making a move to escape. He wasn't. They'd panicked.

There was no one else in the bank. Elmira had been on the way out the front door when the first robber rode in and he had her pinned at gunpoint instantly.

Carmody was unable to intervene. They'd pulled her inside and Carmody started exchanging fire with the six who remained outside.

Carmody had worked his way down from the roof and approached us hat in hand. Literally. His silly little derby was in his hands even though it was pouring.

"I am truly sorry, both of you. But he had Elmira here in his sights as soon as he rode up, and I couldn't risk a shot."

"I'm aware of that, Tom. Keeping your cool saved her life. Thanks."

Elmira said something too but I couldn't understand it because she was spitting mud and hair out of her mouth. But whatever she said it sounded comforting.

"So what do we do?" Carmody asked. "Do we let them go? I believe they'll not be in the mood for hanging around much longer and will be piling out the back door with Spencer and the silver. Last I saw the rest of them was still waiting on the opposite side of the building from us."

I hesitated and Carmody grew impatient.

"We gotta act *now*. You're the damn philosopher," he said. "Are we sticking by the deal or not?"

Elmira made a vague sputtering noise but I ignored her.

"Tom, here's the way I see it," I said. "If they leave the back way and ride west, they'll get bogged down in that delta mud for sure, so that's out. I doubt if they'll want to ride back into town, so I'm guessing they'll ride out to our left and head out the road until they pick up a trail."

I wanted to lament how only in this misbegotten town would someone build a bank at the edge of a swamp, and it did seem like an interesting question to ponder while I avoided a decision, but Carmody looked ready to strangle me.

"I think they'll realize that," I said, "and come around the side and ride and shoot like hell and try to beat it out of here along the road. And they'll keep Spencer for a few miles but he'll have to ride double and slow down one horse so they'll kill him."

I was talking tactics, but whether he knew it or not, Carmody was right about this being a philosophical question. Should I keep a deal with criminals who I suspect have no intention of keeping up their end?

There was an 18th century philosopher named Kant who wrote books that I am sure even glazed over the eyes of other 18th century philosophers, but it he got around to making a point after standing in the rain for half an hour it would be this: If it's wrong to lie to good people it's wrong to lie to bad people, too.

If everybody lets convenience be the determining factor in whether they keep their agreements there's no point in making agreements in the first place.

And for reasons I hadn't had time to explain to Carmody, Spencer's fate was irrelevant.

And then my whole internal monologue became irrelevant as gunshots erupted from the other side of the bank. First a pop, then a few seconds later a roaring volley of pistol and rifle fire.

Carmody was off like a deer, pulling a pistol from his waistband and scooping up his rifle from the pile near the front door. I hoped it still worked, soaked as it was.

I had no choice but to follow. I'd wasted the few precious seconds we had with my thumb stuck up my ass thinking about philosophy and neglected to tell Carmody what Elmira had told me: that the manager was dead and there was no one else in the building.

Carmody was hot to kill outlaws and save lives. And the only life to be saved was one that didn't want to be saved.

Still, the scenario did have some appeal.

So I fished out my wet, slippery Colt out of my holster and ran after him.

Carmody shot the first one who rounded the corner and I hit the second rider in his left eye. I couldn't tell how badly the one Carmody shot was hurt but he slid off to the side as his panicked horse bolted. His foot was caught in the stirrup and if he wasn't dead now he would be dragged to death soon.

By my count that made six men left, plus Spencer. But Spencer had to have been the one who initiated the gunfire, so it was an open question as to whether he was alive and how many robbers he might have killed or wounded.

Both I and Carmody were hugging the left-hand corner of the bank. That would be the closest route for men on horseback to make it to the road, but there was no reason why they couldn't ride around the other side, assuming they could make it through the mud. Also worrisome was the fact that if someone were still inside, the front door could be opened and we could be fired up from there.

So I tried to monitor both directions at once.

A second later I heard sodden hoofbeats behind me and I turned in time to see a horse sink into the mud up to his fetlocks and throw his rider forward. The rider held onto his gun, rolled and came up to one knee and looked like he was ready to shoot but was blown back as he was hit in the chest.

I looked and I realized that Oak had fired his little squirrel gun, but the scenario didn't make sense because I don't think the .22 could have knocked over a tin can.

And then I saw Miller, the old pickle-faced druggist.

He'd shot the rider with a musket. A *flintlock,* of all things. A gun that would have been on the verge of being outdated during the Texas Revolution and had probably hung over his fireplace for thirty years.

But you can't argue with results.

The smoke from the flintlock coiled upward into the rainy dampness and there was dead silence for several minutes until I heard Spencer's voice from inside the bank.

"It's all clear, Hawke. Come in the front door by yourself. There's only one robber left alive and I've got him tied up."

Carmody looked at me and Spencer spoke again.

"I mean it, Hawke. Just you. Send Carmody and the woman back, along with the guys with the peashooter and the musket. It's important that I see you alone for a couple minutes."

Carmody shook his head and I held up a finger.

"Does this still have something to do with your son David?" I asked.

"My son's name was Donald and you're still a clever bastard, but thanks for giving me the chance to tip you off if somebody was holding a gun to my head. I'm fine. I'm alone. I just have some unfinished business with you. Just you."

I looked at Carmody and shrugged.

Then Spencer opened the door wide and spread his arms. I noted that he had a gun, presumably one of the robbers', in his holster. He waved me in, as cordially as a neighbor inviting me for pie and coffee.

I shooed everyone else away and walked in.

The interior was bright with amber lantern-light. Even though it was only a little after five the clouds and rain had imposed an early dusk. Whether the manager had fired the coal lamps up earlier in the day or Spencer had just done it I didn't know and didn't care.

I just wanted this game to be over.

I looked around, and started by poking my head out the back door. All the horses but for two had run off. One was dead. The other, a big roan, chewed absently and peacefully on the few stalks of vegetation that stuck out above the water. The marsh was flooded, and the water had begun to overrun the threshold of the reinforced back door.

The body nearest the door was in water so deep that one of the man's arms floated.

I counted the bodies in the back, in the front room, and by the safe.

"There's no one left alive," I said.

"Only you and I know that. Your story will be that the one that was tied up got loose and shot me and then you killed him."

I stopped and surveyed the carnage.

"Well...shit," I said.

"Yep," he said, coughed into his handkerchief, and sat on the edge of a desk.

"You did your best to get killed but old habits die harder than you do."

"Reflex. Goddamned panicky idiots. I shot one and took his gun and shot one more and the rest peed their pants and went loco. Some of them shot the others by accident. Everybody was dead before I knew it. Dead before I *wanted* them to be."

"It would have been a good way to die, wouldn't it? Would have looked good in the papers."

"I ain't ashamed to say that's important to me," Spencer said, and coughed again.

It'd be important to me, too, I told him.

Spencer seemed to look past me into the distance.

"You know, I never did hold it against you what you did to my boy. But a lot of folks felt I should have held it against you, and they thought less of me because I never did nothing about it."

"So you figured you'd kill two birds with one stone, so to speak, with one of them being you. Your last earthly act would be to take vengeance on the man who killed your son. But you're getting along in years, so no shame in losing the draw. A noble way to go. Befitting an aging gunfighter."

"Especially as I would have been killed by the lawman with the lightning draw, although at the time I had no way of knowing you'd earn that reputation."

I almost laughed but I was now thoroughly tired of his bullshit and wanted to get this over.

"I get it, Jake. I saw the blood you coughed up into your handkerchief while you were in the cell. I'm guessing you've got consumption and think it's going to kill you and want to take the easy way out."

"It *ain't* easy," he roared.

And then he calmed a bit.

"And it ain't consumption. Doctor thinks it's what he calls a tumor. A growth, way down deep in one of my lungs. Says he's seen the kind I got before, and a *slow, painful death is inevitable*. Those was his words: *A slow, painful death is inevitable*. I'm not scared of the pain nor the death, but I sure as hell don't want what I wind up being before I die to be what people remember after I'm gone."

I couldn't argue with that. My grandfather had lost his faculties for the last decade of his life and to this day he's remembered around my hometown as the crazy old man who talked to himself and got lost in his own neighborhood. Not the man who built a sawmill or raised five children after his wife died or commanded a unit in 1812. He was fixed in everybody's mind as the crazy old man who talked to himself.

"I understand that part," I told Spencer. "But why me? And did you stop to think that I'd have to live with your killing?"

"You was handy, that's all. I'd been in Austin and heard tell of the troubles here and how many men you'd planted. Figured you'd be pretty damn quick, you wouldn't hesitate, and probably wouldn't even recognize me, the way I look now."

I waited him out for the rest of the answer.

"And no, I'm sorry, I did not think about your feelings. You'll get over it. I've seen you get over plenty. And you do owe me."

"You talk like you still expect me to kill you," I said. "I'm not in the business of mercy killing."

"Suppose I draw on you right now?"

"You won't draw. I mean, maybe you'd draw but you won't shoot me. I don't think you'd do it because you know it's wrong, and I know you won't do it because you've got common sense. You'd still be in the same predicament but worse if you kill me and stay alive."

That sounded good and I believed it myself but I still harbored a shade of doubt.

"You say you're not in the business of mercy killing," he said, "but you'll put down an injured horse. I seen you do that plenty. You felt bad for the animals. Wouldn't you feel bad for me? Suppose I was being tortured by Indians and you couldn't save me but could end it with a gunshot. Wouldn't you kill me then?"

"It's not the same thing," I said, and I was right, but no two things are *ever* the same and knew I was trying to argue my way out the easy way, and Spencer knew it too.

"Supposing I was in a burning building and was going to roast alive. Would you kill me then?"

And then he picked up the burning coal-oil lamp from the desk and smashed it on the ground.

"I said I wasn't scared of pain," he said as the flaming liquid spread in tendrils like flickering fingers, moving in a nasty, alive way. "I lied. I'm scared right now. I'm scared of what it will feel like to burn alive."

The flames spread to a wastepaper basket and ignited some of the papers hanging over the edge.

"I'm a Catholic," he said, raising his voice over the crackle of the flames. "Suicide is a sin, and I truly believe that if I die by my own hand I'll burn like this for eternity."

And then he drew and shot a hole in a lantern on the counter. It spun crazily and landed on the floor, its wick still burning and the oil catching fire with a chuffing sound.

I thought about trying to pull him out of the room. As sick as he was, he still looked like he could put up a fight and I wasn't eager to burn for even a minute, much less an eternity.

What I don't know about fires is considerable, except for the fact that I don't like them, and I didn't know if the flames would spread into an inferno or if this grand drama would end with some scorched curtains and a pile of burnt rubbish and a still-breathing Jake Spencer hatching another plot to make me kill him.

I had a decision to make, and I *do* know a little about that process. I saw a lot of decisions, good and bad, made during battle.

Sometimes those choices were made after long and careful deliberation.

Sometimes they are made quickly as a result of fear or anger.

And sometimes, maybe most of the time, they are simply the culmination of pure exhaustion.

I gave up and shot Jake Spencer in the forehead.

I told Carmody and Elmira the truth, of course, and they assured me that I'd done the right thing, both from a moral and practical standpoint.

Moral because I'd ended a man's suffering. I wasn't so sure about that, but I knew I'd get over it. Spencer was right. I always did.

Practical because the damned bank burned to the ground within half an hour, despite the best efforts of the local bucket brigade. It occurred to me that I needed to figure out some better method of fighting fires in town. Maybe, too, there were laws that existed, or ones that I could make up, to keep wood buildings in town from being such deathtraps.

I told everybody else the story Spencer had concocted about the tied-up prisoner escaping and shooting him. I added an embellishment or two about stray shots hitting the lamps. I don't know if people believed my story but seeing as how there was not much left of the place but ashes, bones, and a charred, empty safe I didn't expect anyone to check the sequence of events too carefully.

The good news was that the silver and the cash from the bank were recovered out in back, underneath one of the bodies. The silver was on the stage the next day and I laid the cash out on the cot in the cell to let it dry. I left it there for a while, figuring it was as safe a place as any, until we could come up with a new bank.

That won't be as hard as I'd expected. The safe still works fine even though the paint is peeled off. We just have to find a new building and some strong men to carry the safe.

It turned out that the robbers were a gang that had in the past achieved some notoriety — even admiration — for bold daylight robberies, a fact that further diminished my opinion of gangs in particular and of mankind in general.

Worse, the Dead Horse Hill paper got wind of what happened, rearranged the facts a might, and called me a "human Gatling gun."

I gradually unwound in the quiet week that followed, spending what time I could sequestered in my office or my room at the lodging house, hiding out from people who wanted to talk about that newspaper story. After a few days I began spending some time in the Spoon and playing the piano well into the night.

Carmody continued to amaze me with his knowledge of things that I just can't imagine how he knows. One night I slipped in some Beethoven, a nice rousing part of the beginning of the Third Symphony that could pass for a frontier ballad if you sped it up a little.

"That's the one Beethoven called *Eroica*," Carmody said. "But like you usually do, you cowpoked-it up a might."

"How the hell do you know all this stuff?" I asked. "For a guy that grew up eating squirrels you sure have an unusual depth of knowledge."

"I ain't no dummy, Josiah. I go to a concert now and then when I'm traveling through a city. I read some whenever I get a chance."

I could tell what was coming and dreaded it.

Carmody, well into his second bottle of whiskey, started wagging that finger and lecturing me.

"That ditty you're playing was originally named after Napoleon. You heard of him?"

His twang always broadened when he was lubricated. It came out: *Yuh heeeeered-a-him?*

I was not in a subtle mood when I replied and confirmed that yes, indeed, I had *heeeered-a-him.*

"Old Ludwig tore up the dedication page and changed the name of the whole damn piece of music," Carmody continued, "When Napoleon declared himself Emperor."

I steeled myself for whatever little lesson Carmody would not be able to restrain himself from imparting.

"You remember that things did not turn out well for the little emperor after he got too full of himself," he lectured.

His expression turned serious.

"My point is that me and Elmira and even a few of the in-bred locals in this town have grown sorta used to you – kind of *fond* of you in a way — and don't want to see nothing happen to you now that you are sporting that lightning draw and them furious fists and have become a human fucking Gatling gun."

"I appreciate that."

"And I sincerely mean *no offense* when I tell you that a comeuppance can happen to any man when he gets cocky."

"No offense taken," I said.

"What I'm trying to say is, the worst thing can happen to a man is when he starts believing his own bullshit."

"I agree," I said.

"But I don't think that will happen. You are by nature a modest man."

"That's true," I said.

"All right, that's off my chest. Now let's hear some bar-room Mozart. I daresay you are one of the best piano players I ever did hear."

"Nah, I'm not that good," I lied.

And then I cowpoked-up *The Marriage of Figaro*.

THE END

THE MOUNTAIN — OF SLOW MADNESS

A HAWKE & CARMODY
WESTERN SHORT STORY

CARL DANE

RAGING BULL PUBLISHING

It wasn't the first time I'd seen an abandoned child riding alone on horseback through open country. Over the years I'd seen dozens, I would guess, clinging to the reins, headed to no particular destination – generally following whatever whim the horse dictated — after their homes were devastated by artillery fire, or their families killed in Indian raids.

But I'd never seen any child in such a state of soul-blasted shock.

She appeared to be ten or so. Her eyes were too big for her face and despite the white-hot glare of an August sun, she hardly blinked. She wouldn't look at me when I shouted from a distance, nor when I trotted toward her head-on, slowly, taking pains not to move abruptly.

At first glance, the girl didn't appear to be wounded or beat up – not on the outside, anyway. She was covered with trail dust and her hair hung in loose yellow coils down the front of her face, but she wasn't badly sunburned and her lips weren't cracked from thirst. Her horse, a stocky and nondescript mustang that looked like what you'd expect to find on a small farm, didn't look spent, and in fact seemed content. The breed, half-wild no matter how hard you try to domesticate them, can generally find their own food and water without human intervention and often display better survival skills than their riders.

My deputy, Tom Carmody, had spotted the horse and rider when they crested a small hill more than a mile from town. He'd been sitting on the bench in front of the marshal's office whittling and spitting tobacco juice and generating the daily reincarnation of the mess that he creates everywhere.

But suddenly, he caught movement in the distance and went on point like a hound.

"Shit," he said, "there's somebody in trouble."

It came out *shee-it, thar's somebody in trebble.*

Carmody is from the hills of Eastern Tennessee, where he grew up eating squirrels and drinking liquor made out of feed scraps fermented in tin buckets. Now he favors vested suits and elegant bowlers and looks exactly like a squirrel-eating mountain man wearing a suit and a bowler to a costume party.

I'd deputized Carmody about a year-and-a-half ago when I came to this one-lung little Texas Hill Country town to figure out who killed the former marshal, Billy Gannon, who'd been captain of my unit during the war. Gannon had left word that it something happened to him to find me and I'd set things straight.

Something did happen. Gannon was ambushed by a gunfighter and shot four times in the head. And I did resolve the matter by finding the man who'd done it and killing him.

In the process I inherited Gannon's job and Tom Carmody.

Carmody had been languishing in a cell, charged with beating up a dozen men who apparently badly deserved it, and I gave him a choice of staying in jail or becoming my deputy.

After citing his constitutional protections against cruel and unusual punishment, he took me up on my offer.

And in case you're wondering, he beat up the dozen men all at the same time.

Carmody watched the rider's progress for a minute or so and noted that the horse was wandering in an aimless fashion. He could somehow make out that it was ridden by a very small woman or a child. I could barely discern the shape of a horse. It could have been a mule, a cow, or an anteater for all I could tell.

Carmody sees and hears things normal men can't. He'd been a scout during the war, and while I never knew him back then I later learned he'd been something of a legend for the way he could read tracks and terrain.

I never was much of a track-reader.

But I'm very good at reading people and situations, and was a lieutenant in a unit that specialized in what you would characterize as acts of creative subterfuge or dirty tricks, depending on whether you were doing the acts or having them done to you.

Let me back up a little. My name is Josiah Hawke. I'd joined the Sixth Illinois Cavalry after an undistinguished three-year career teaching philosophy at a small college, where I'd lectured halfheartedly about topics like conflict and violence.

I guess you'd say that when I had a chance to put theory into practice during the war I found my true calling.

After hostilities ceased I made a half-hearted return to my half-hearted career, and lasted exactly one month.

A strongman and boxer with a traveling show goaded me into a fight one night, calling me out in front of a group of friends and students. He offered me ten-to-one odds if I could stay in the ring with him for two rounds. He was strong and quick but I'd spend four years in a special unit fighting with any weapon available to me, including my head — *especially* my head — and I was able to figure out his moves in less than a minute and dropped him with a crisp and infinitely satisfying cross to the point of his chin.

Suckers in the audience at a traveling show aren't supposed to know how to counter-punch so the pug took exception to my tactic. When he got to his feet he clinched and tried to gouge my eye out.

I took *strong* exception to that, so I beat him to death.

I didn't set out to kill him, but I didn't exercise much restraint in the process of administering his lesson, either, and when it became apparent that he wasn't going to get up – ever – I hustled out of town a few steps ahead of the law.

In the next few years I traveled the country, picking up bareknuckle bouts here and there, and doing some gunwork, mostly as a lawman.

Carmody had enjoyed a shorter career in lawing, but in the time we'd been together he'd saved my life more than I'd saved his, which is why I put up with his wood shavings, gobs of tobacco-spit, and his endless homespun analysis of things that don't really merit discussion by normal people.

But now I sensed something new in him, something strange and alien. He knew, and I knew, that the situation with the horse on the hill required only one lawman to handle, so he made no effort to move. Just a few weeks ago he'd have been riding out there by now and scolding me over his shoulder about how I was slowing with age.

But he remained planted on the bench, holding the stick he was whittling in a left hand that was resting on his leg, a hand attached to an arm that doesn't seem to work very well since he took a bullet on that side during a rescue raid we staged a few months ago.

Carmody leaned back and looked down with that resigned look old men display when they give up — sort of an apology flashed by the eyes followed by a quick, diverted look away. It was the type of attitude I'd seen my grandfather betray when a variety of maladies finally overtook him at age 70 or so and he resigned himself to spending his days in a chair.

Actually, Carmody didn't know exactly how old he was – they didn't keep much in the way of records where he came from – but his best guess was 43.

So I mounted my big Steeldust, which I kept hitched outside the office, and rode off, leaving Carmody to whittle yet another point on another stick.

I calculated that rider's horse would more or less follow the contours of the trail that led to the road into town, so I set off at an angle that would intercept the route and allow me to approach with a full view of the landscape above the rider, just in case there was trouble following.

I didn't expect trouble.

Nor did I expect a little girl with impossibly wide eyes that opened a window into a mind blasted hollow with horror.

What I don't know about children is basically everything, so I turned the girl over to my sometime girlfriend, Elmira Adler, who owns the Silver Spoon, a local bar and bordello. Elmira inherited the place from her late husband, her daughter's step-father. Her daughter murdered her step-father, and he deserved it, but that's a story for another time. Elmira, therefore, is something of an expert on problem children.

She is also quite direct. She led the girl to a chair, sat her down, looked right into those huge eyes, and yelled, "Hello?"

Elmira shook her head.

"Nothing in there," she said.

"I found her coming down the slope that leads down to the delta," I said. "I couldn't spend a lot of time backtrailing but all I saw were single tracks, so I don't think she was being pursued. Not lately, anyway."

I reached over and brushed back her hair from her face.

"It's about eleven now, and she's a little red from the sun but not burnt, and from the looks of her she doesn't spend much time outside in the first place, so if she'd been a long time in the saddle she'd be baked like a potato for sure. So, to me that means she wasn't on the trail yesterday, which was also cloudless. But she's covered with trail dust, more than you get from a couple hours in the saddle, so I'd say she started out sometime late yesterday and rode through the night."

Elmira fetched the girl a glass of water. She drank it wordlessly, expressionlessly, and gently set the glass down on the table.

Elmira stood with her arms crossed, brow gently knitted in a pattern of fine, barely detectable lines. She's no kid. I don't know her age either. Unlike Carmody she probably knows her age but I'm afraid to ask, so I've always pegged in the same range as me and Carmody, early 40s.

What wrinkles she has look more like the fine engraving from the image of a coin instead of the claw-marks frontier life ravages into the face of many in her profession.

For whatever reason, that's always how I thought of her – a woman made out of precious metal, a silvery image framed in golden hair that was streaked with platinum.

Elmira's eyes are as wide as the little girl's and just as innocent, even though Elmira – who had been taken by the Apaches as a child and entered the life of a bar dove and a bordello madam after she escaped – had surely seen it all.

Or almost all.

Probably not what had made this girl shut her mind down.

"Hello?" Elmira waved her hand in front of the girl's face and then leaned in close.

"Anybody in there?"

Frustrated, she retrieved a piece of cake from in back of the bar and set it in front of the girl, who ate it mechanically, without haste or apparent enjoyment.

"She needs a doctor," Elmira said.

We don't have a regular doctor in town. There was a disheveled little man who rides through once a week and tends to whatever maladies have arisen. He calls himself a doctor, although rumor has it he also treats farm animals.

Towns like my adopted home of Shadow Valley don't have much in the way of services and rely on whomever we can get to ride a circuit and visit from time to time – doctors, judges, preachers, and undertakers.

We still don't have an undertaker; the old one died more than a year ago and we've never been able to find one willing to come our way. As town marshal, the job of disposing of dead bodies falls to me.

That's probably a good check and balance in the system because I do my share to provide the supply.

But in the year-and-a-half I've been here, Shadow Valley has made considerable progress. We have a new bank, built after I burned the old one down – again, a story for another time – along with several new shops, and, as of this week, an auditorium that will serve as a combination church and theater.

"The doctor comes this way in a couple of days," I said, "assuming he's not tied up on a ranch somewhere getting cattle ready for the fall drives. She doesn't seem hurt or sick, at least in the conventional sense. Whatever she's got goes deeper than that. And I can't afford the time to take her somewhere."

Elmira fixed me with her look of reproach – she does that by tilting her head and raising an eyebrow – and I could see she wasn't grasping the gravity of the situation.

"Look," I said, "I could take her to the doctor in Dead Horse Hill but the ride will tie me up for most of the day. And right now it's important that I shake Carmody out of his coma so we start backtracking the girl to find out where she came from."

She still didn't get it and spread her arms, palms-up.

"Why?"

"Because I've seen the look on her face before. It's the look kids get when they've seen their family killed or their house burned down. There's something at the beginning of her trail that I need to deal with. Soon. There could be others in danger. And I need to start *now*."

The eyebrow arched a little higher, as it does in her continuum from mild to moderate reproach.

"You promised me you'd go to church. The first service is a very big day for the town — and for me. We need you there, an official presence, especially since Carmody won't come because he's a church-hater."

I shook my head.

"Carmody doesn't 'hate' church. He was a chaplain during the war. Not an official one, but lots of units had men of faith fill in when there wasn't a real chaplain assigned to the unit. Carmody was a lay preacher back home. And I believe him. He can quote Bible stuff by chapter and verse. But he says what he saw the war kicked the faith out of him and he's done with Bible-thumping."

She arched her eyebrow to maximum reproach status, to the point where it looked as though it actually might hurt to bend it that far.

"All I know," she said, "is that half the people in this town have gone into hock to build the church and hire a minister and it's important for the future of the town that you show up."

Elmira was right about the future of the town, I think.

You see, until there's some anchor to a community, towns like Shadow Valley tend to remain way stations for drifters. Among the drifting crowd, about half the population is made up of criminals and the other half by victims and they do their damndest to get together whenever possible.

That provides job security for people like me and Carmody – and maybe the town gun-smith – but normal folk, the kind we'd actually *like* to attract, need schools, hospitals, and the like. And, for Shadow Valley and other towns in ass-end territories of the West, the church is usually the seedling for the growth of those branches of civilization.

So I agreed to delay my departure for a couple of hours and hustle over to the service, which would begin in fifteen minutes or there-abouts, given fifteen minutes in either direc-tion. All times here are more or less collective hunches as we set our timepieces to the clock in front of the bank, which the bank manager sets to what he guesses is noon by a quick glance to make sure the sun is sort of overhead, which seems to me to be rather inexact science.

We had nowhere to leave the stunned lit-tle girl so Elmira took her by the hand and led her inside the church. I noticed as we walked in that it still smelled of sawdust.

She would probably do nothing except stare blankly and catatonically for the next hour. I couldn't hold that against her. In my in-frequent visits to churches I'd generally done more or less the same.

So she marched mechanically between the pews until she saw the tall bearded man with the clerical collar and the frock coat and then she pointed at him and screamed.

"It's him! It's him! It's him!"

She shrieked like a machine, seemingly without stopping for air, like some sort of piston engine.

Elmira, in a whisper that seemed oddly unnecessary in contrast to the howling, told me to stay put while she took care of the girl, and she slung her over her shoulder like a sack of flour and left.

We could hear the screams fade into the distance, unceasing.

The circuit-riding preacher was flustered by the incident but like most of us he had a job to do and he did it, nonstop.

When the preacher did take an infrequent breath, I could hear the screams, faintly, probably from inside the Spoon, as I sat staring blankly and catatonically for what was probably one hour but felt like four.

It had been pretty dry for two weeks and some of the trails had become hard as stone. I never could have followed the tracks of the girl's horse.

I'm actually not a bad tracker and in fact I am skilled enough to know what I don't know. I know enough to let Carmody do it for me.

"Them wildflowers up ahead been rode through," he said, jerking his head. "They're all sparkly-like in the sun. That's the tell-tale when they been mashed on. Can you see that?"

"Of course," I lied. "Plain as day."

Carmody and I had decided to start tracking right after I spoke to the circuit preacher, Reverend William Julian, who was cooperative but apparently genuinely befuddled and also distracted. He was on his way to yet another service.

The man must have had lungs made of leather.

In any event, the Reverend Julian said he was mystified by the girl's reaction; he'd never seen her, he told me, and had no clue as to why she would yell, "it's him."

The girl wasn't shedding much light on the issue, either, because even though she'd stopped screaming she'd clammed up.

I made a note to check out Julian's alibi but there seemed little point. He'd ridden in from the opposite direction from a nearby town where he'd said he'd delivered an early-morning service and would complete the circuit with an evening service two hours to the north. Elmira had known his schedule when she'd engaged him through the bishop, so what he said checked out.

Whether he was actually at each service is something so easily verified I'm not sure anyone would try to fake it, but I figured I'd go through the motions when the telegraph office opened the next day.

Carmody and I rode for three hours in fits and starts. He'd regained a little of his fire now that he was on the hunt. When the trail disappeared Carmody would scout the possible branches in search of a miniscule bent branch, faint tracks near a stream where the horse stopped to drink, or leaves that had become infinitesimally matted by hoof prints.

When we reached the foot of a vast sunbaked hill – or maybe it was a mountain, I've never been quite sure where the dividing line is in the definition — Carmody dismounted and without explanation flopped flat on his stomach.

I noticed he winced as he put some weight on his left arm. I'd also noticed that he'd been holding the reins in his right hand only for the entire trip.

Carmody inexplicably stayed prone.

"Some sort of ritual?" I asked.

"I know you was a fancy officer and all that," Carmody said, a little distracted and more than a little annoyed, "but frankly, in the woods or the open country or anywhere where there ain't a fucking bar and piano you're about as useful as tits on a boar hog."

I wanted to ask what exactly a boar hog was but it would only give him more ammunition to use against me.

In fairness, he had a point. I'd done my share of outdoor reconnoitering in battle but the tactics I chose were always based on the observations of men like Carmody, who I assume were born with innate skill.

I don't think being an outdoorsman is something that can be learned. It's like being six feet tall. You either are or you aren't and if you're not there's absolutely nothing you can do about it.

At least I'm tall.

He grunted as he regained his footing and I noticed that he actually glared at his withering arm with anger, hating at it as though it was a separate entity that had somehow betrayed him.

"Faint tracks going uphill – you can't see them when you look down from horseback," he said. "But from a real sharp angle they stand out. I'd invite you to get down on your belly and see for yourself but you'd probably get lost trying to find your way back up to your horse."

I let it pass.

"I can see where she came from up on the crest, and if I remember right there's a settlement over the ridge. Follow in back of me."

I nodded.

"You *can* follow the ass end of my horse, can't you?"

I let it pass too, but as I sometimes do, I debated the wisdom of my carrying a gun in his presence.

"I mean, it is a pretty small horse," he said. "I'll go slow."

He rode about a hundred feet in front of me. I actually did fall behind because the ground grew increasingly steep and rocky and my horse had trouble with the footing. I favor a breed called a Steeldust, named because they were originally a metallic gray but they now come in pretty much any color. They're as fast as any horse alive in the quarter mile and they're all lungs and long legs. But they're not meant for rough terrain.

Carmody has a stable of horses, several of which he won playing cards, but he favors a small breed called a mountain horse. They are fearless and surefooted as goats but not bred for hauling big loads. Carmody is about six-five and has one of those mountain-man builds with wide shoulders and thick arms with ropey veins and huge hands and wrists.

I would put Carmody at 235. I could see that he'd gained five pounds since being wounded. I can tell a man's weight within a pound or two, a skill I'd picked up as a bareknuckle fighter. I can also read the distance between two men on a street to a foot, and I can come within ten feet or so when gauging a long rifle shot.

Reading distances is a skill I picked up on the battlefield and honed in the following decade as a lawman and a magnet for a mostly deceased breed of morons who feel compelled to shoot at me.

It was a long ride up the hill and I was too far in back to talk so I spent the time thinking about what would happen to Carmody if his arm didn't heal up. He could still shoot and fight with one hand – he certainly wouldn't be the first one-armed lawman in the West – but I wondered if his heart would stay in it. If your heart's not in a fight, your head isn't either, and that condition turns a lawman's job into slow-motion suicide.

I have to admit that I thought about my future as part of the equation, too. I would surely be on the wrong side of the grass by now if not for whatever bone Carmody has in his head that allows him to sniff trouble in the air, find water anywhere – I think he could find it on the moon, if he had to – and wend his way in and out of baffling and vast geography.

My musings were interrupted when the wind shifted and the smell hit us a few hundred feet from the top of the ridge. Burnt wood, sharp, acrid.

Suddenly, Carmody held out his right hand, palm facing me. He stood up on the stirrups, surveyed what I took to be a level spot at the top of the crest, and guided the horse back down toward me.

He was moving slowly, with some stealth, and I didn't need to be told not to move or shout out.

Carmody didn't speak until our mounts were nose-to-nose.

"I only got one hand, and I can use my sidearm in a hurry if I have to, but you'll want your long-gun. We're back to playing your kind of game now."

It was a fertile garden of carnage. Body-parts were scattered among the remains of the town, and many of the buildings were missing roofs or corners that had been consumed by fire.

The scene was a panoramic horror. To the left, there was a severed leg lying beneath what looked like a piece of gutter stuck in the ground like a stake; to the right, a head gaped from atop a pile of bricks and twisted window casings. In front of me were shattered plates, scattered playing cards, and a dollar bill fluttering across a dusty road in a palsied, stop-and-go pattern, like a wounded moth.

Carmody and I had circled in opposite directions, not knowing if any hostiles were hiding in the ruined buildings. We made three revolutions in a tightening spiral, closing in on the center.

I entered all the barns and dwellings and shops and did a search as best I could. Carmody covered me from the outside, alert to anyone bolting from the rubble.

There was no one left alive that I could find, friend or foe.

"This was a little settlement of maybe fifteen people, as I remember," Carmody said. "People mainly kept to themselves but a lot of folk up here are related and come from other towns. There's more places like this deeper in the mountain range."

"Do you have any idea what could set something like this off?"

"None," Carmody said. "I've heard people up here is weird – that some of them, but not all, belong to some strange sect — but never heard of no violence from these parts."

He shook his head and slapped the pommel in frustration and disbelief.

"This ain't nothing I've ever seen. Nothing I've ever *dreamed*. This ain't an Indian raid, ain't a feud, ain't nothing but fucking insanity."

"Shit, the bodies were hacked to pieces, and the buildings torn apart to damn near their individual molecules," I said, realizing that I wasn't telling Carmody anything he couldn't see plainly with his own eyes. Maybe I just wanted to confirm that he saw it too. That I wasn't hallucinating.

"Yep, it's for real," Carmody said, reading my mind. "You ain't dreaming, neither. It's a nightmare, all right. But we're awake."

He cut his eyes over toward the biggest pile of rubble.

"That weren't here before," he said. "Fresh nailed *after* it burned. You can see the hammer marks in the wood."

Stuck in a pile of bricks and doors was a rudely shaped cross made of charred beams from a pulverized building.

We organized the bodyparts into matching piles. From the gruesome reconstruction we learned three things. First, a total of eight adults and two children had been butchered. Second, their killers had been in an extended, methodical rage; much of the dismemberment had required considerable time and many hacking blows, possibly by crude cutting tools like axes or hatchets, judging by the ragged and jagged edges of wounds and the fact that the bones had been pulverized and not cut cleanly. Third, the torsos had not begun to decompose or swell but were stiff and had a purplish hue that lightened just a bit when I pressed hard with my thumb.

That meant, I figured, that the butchery had occurred between eighteen and twenty-four hours ago.

That would coincide with my theory about the girl: She'd somehow escaped the carnage, grabbed a horse, and set off to...well, anywhere but *here*.

And while it was more guesswork, I reckoned that the carnage must have involved a dozen people or more in on the rampage. Reducing several buildings to shards and foundations is labor-intensive and would have been a challenge to even a boatload of the most psychotic Vikings.

But *why?*

"Maybe four hours of sun left," Carmody said, interrupting my circular train of thought, removing his bowler, and wiping his forehead with the back of his hand.

I took his point. We could either head back to Shadow Valley and attempt to get more help or try to track whoever had orchestrated this carnage. Tracking would be easy; even I could follow what I assumed would be a large gang on horseback.

But what would we do when we found them? Improvise, I guess.

It wouldn't be the first time we'd cracked the eggs first and then worried about how to bake the cake.

I nodded.

Carmody nodded back, and we headed north up a steep mountain path.

Up ahead, I could see the shimmer of some trampled wildflowers.

"When we catch up to whatever bunch of locos did this," Carmody said as we followed an obvious trail of hoofprints that Carmody said would not be a challenge for a blind mule walking backward, "there's gonna be much wailing and gnashing of teeth."

"Don't forget that we might be the ones doing the wailing," I said. "And you're in an unusually biblical mood today."

Carmody smiled with his lips but not his eyes.

"Trouble always follows religion, don't it? Within a couple hours of our first visit from a preacher we got a massacre on our hands."

"That's a little harsh," I said. "There's no connection between the two as far as I can see. That reverend couldn't possibly have…"

"I ain't talking about him in *specific*," Carmody said, cutting me off. "I just mean the general notion that wherever there's religion there's blood and guts all over the place, either before, after, or during. Sometimes the religion's an excuse to do it. Sometimes we promise people we'll pray for them and I guess that makes them braver and that means they get killed easier or do *their* killing more efficient-like."

I nodded.

"I'm not agreeing or disagreeing with you," I said, "but I know what you're saying. History shows plenty of killing done in the name of religion."

Carmody said nothing, so I asked the question that was on both our minds.

"You're talking about that cross?"

"*Course* I'm talking about that cross," he said. "Could be somebody put it up as a plea for divine intervention during the massacre, but that's a stretch. More likely whoever did the deed stuck it there like planting a flag."

"What do you think it means?"

"Trouble," Carmody said.

And we rode for a while in silence.

I let the subject drop.

Religion is a touchy subject, even with Carmody. *Especially* with Carmody.

I didn't know exactly what had happened to him during the war, but I suspected he'd soured on the concept after leading services for men who were subsequently chopped up in battle, or saying prayers for wounded who suffered and died.

He'd always been tight-lipped about it, even when he was drinking and sticking his finger in the air and lecturing me about whatever subject happened to enter what was left of his mind at two in the morning.

We'd talked about religion only once before, at least in any sustained way, when I played *Be Thou My Vision* near closing time at the Spoon. Elmira has an upright that's in pretty good shape and oddly, even after a decade of hammering my fists against all species of hard heads, my hands still work the ivories pretty well.

The problem is that I get bored with the same old dance-hall music and make use of whatever tends to be floating through my head, which often includes Beethoven, Mozart, or the type of music that was endlessly in camp, including the dittys and the hymns.

Give it a good steady beat and anything sounds good to a drunken trail-hand.

Carmody had astonishing recall of the sources of what he called my "cowpoked-up" classics and whenever I'd question him about how in hell he knew so much he'd get a little vague and tell me that he might look a little rough he'd been to a concert or two.

One night he picked up on my interpretation of *Be Thou My Vision* and, after lecturing me on the contributions of his Irish ancestors, who, he said, wrote it centuries ago, he sang along for five verses.

The assorted riff-raff hadn't been aware that the lilting ballad I was pounding out was a hymn and seemed in danger of leaving when Carmody – well into his second quart of whiskey – energized the late-night crowd by asking the roughest-looking ones at the bar what their religion was.

Carmody responded to each answer by saying, "that's nice, but it ain't my religion," followed by, "burn in hell, heretic," and one old man laughed so hard he couldn't catch his breath.

But when we were helping clean up after tossing the drunks out for the night he turned serious and told me a little about being an "informal" chaplain during the war. He wasn't commissioned but had been a lay preacher in Tennessee and knew the drill.

He'd been a young man during the war but, Carmody said, a lot of soldiers were really just kids, away from home for the first time, and the chaplain was sort of a father to them.

That's where it ended, and I noticed that Carmody wasn't smiling when we locked the doors.

The tracks led us up a steep pass.

My horse was not happy with the incline and the jagged terrain. Carmody's overgrown pony was handling the obstacles all right but beginning to sag.

This time we heard the next town instead of smelling it.

In mountain country like this, you can be on top of something before you know it and when we crested we could see about 20 people, men, women, and a few children, walking toward the center of the small settlement, converging like iron filings drawn to a magnet.

We could hear the scuffling of their boots on the hard-baked clay. Other than that, there wasn't much noise. No conversation. In the distance, a dog barked.

A few of the men and women looked back at us as we rode into town. They didn't seem overtly hostile, and that actually complicated our task. If we'd been met by angry men shooting we could have responded in kind.

Right now, the only option seemed to be to circle the town and get our bearings and then ride into the center of this knot of men, women, and children and try to find someone to talk to about what happened in the next town over and why tracks from a drove of horses led to this spot.

At least that's what I was anticipating when I was shot.

I heard the crack of the gun a heartbeat after I felt the searing pain across my shoulder blades. The grazing impact sent me a little sideways. I figured the best course of action would be to roll off the horse, draw, and keep rolling.

In the fraction of a second I had to think I guessed that the bullet had come from my left side had grazed me across the back of my shoulders. I'd heard no crunching or cracking, which was a good sign, but I could feel a hot wetness spreading across my back.

When I hit the ground I rolled like a log a couple times, hoping to make myself an elusive target. I could hear guns being cocked and male voices telling me, and presumably Carmody also, to freeze.

I had my revolver clear of the holster and was ready to finish more roll and come up firing when the ground disappeared.

It seemed like an impossible joke: I'd suddenly found myself suspended in mid-air. And then I realized I'd rolled myself off a damn cliff and I wasn't floating but was hurtling to-ward some branches below – *way* below – with alarming speed.

The mind works in odd ways and as I fell into the abyss I used what may have been my last few seconds on earth debating whether to keep the revolver in my hand. If I somehow survived the fall I'd need it, but if I landed with it after surviving a fall I could shoot myself by accident when I made impact.

And then my rumination was interrupted by a tree branch that struck me in the stomach. It was from some sort of bouncy evergreen and it gave enough that while I was winded I wasn't badly hurt.

I dropped the gun to free up both hands and hugged that branch like my Momma. The branch bent, and I ripped off needles as I fell, but I was slowing myself down even though I was losing some skin in the process.

I could hear the needles tear as they slid through my arms and hands and could smell the sharp pine tang as I stripped the needles from the tree.

Then I heard the gun strike the ground below. It didn't go off, which would have been an inconvenience as it would alert the men above to my position, and it was in some ways reassuring because I knew that there was some sort of nearby surface between me and the abyss.

And then I hit that surface.

Hard.

I had the wind knocked out of me, literally. I'd heard myself forced to exhale when I hit and now I couldn't seem to breathe in at all.

So I lay there listening to myself not breathing while voices above shouted that I'd gone down the side and they'd either have to come looking for me or saturate the hill with gunfire until they were sure I was dead.

I managed to suck in a little air and scrambled to my knees and looked down and was immediately sorry that I did. I was on an outcropping not much more than four feet wide and below was a sheer drop that stretched into what basically looked like infinity.

Without really knowing why, I pulled my knees to my chest and slid between the cliff wall and a big rock.

Or maybe it was a boulder. I've never been able to figure out the difference. Pushing with my legs I was able to rock it a couple of inches, and then a foot, and then it grudgingly rolled over the precipice and headed into the abyss.

It made a lot of noise and struck something at least five times on the way down before landing with a concussive splash.

Voices from above concluded that if I'd hit that water I must be dead.

And then my brain kicked in and realized my body had done the right thing, acting on instinct.

I would have patted myself on the back except it would have hurt like hell. There was a burning streak from shoulder to shoulder that felt like the welt of a whip and the blood was trickling down the small of my back.

But I had to get back up and find Carmody and then figure out what on earth was going on.

When my unit was taught climbing maneuvers during the war it was drilled into us that you never trust a "vegetable hold." Meaning that you never pulled yourself up by grabbing a plant.

That always struck me as dubious advice because the steep parts of nature don't come equipped with convenient stone handles. But my little piece of outdoor hell did feature exposed tree roots growing out of the slope, so I had the vegetative equivalent of a rope ladder and my two trips up were fairly straightforward.

I made two trips because my fall had knocked both the wind and the sense out of me and I'd forgotten to look for the gun until I was almost to the top, so I had to climb back down. I found it, partially covered by branches and pine needles. And then it occurred to me, as I regained more of my senses, that the shape of the revolver pretty closely matched a painful bruise on my short ribs.

I'd landed on the damn thing.

I forced myself to sit down on the ledge for a few minutes and try to get my wits about me. There comes a time when, no matter how urgent your mission, you need to take some time to get over what rattled your brain and clear your head. Otherwise you can wind up shooting the wrong people. Or, in my case, you could walk into a gunfight with nothing to shoot with because you'd forgotten to pick up your gun.

After five minutes I could almost take in a full breath, although the rib didn't make the process pleasant. My field of vision had expanded from little gray tunnels to something approximating a normal field of view, although I still saw some sparkles around the edges.

The second trip up was easy, and I'd almost made it to the top when I almost shot the kid.

He'd poked his head over the edge and asked me if I needed a hand.

I instinctively let loose of my vegetable hold and went for my gun and lost my grip and almost suffered the same fate as the boulder. When I finally regained my hold on a tree root I was enraged and sputtering and resigned to the fact that if this boy, who looked to be about ten, was going to kill me or find some others to kill me there was absolutely nothing I could do about it.

"We're not supposed to use words like that, Mister," the boy said, grabbing a handful of my shirt and pulling as I heaved myself back to level ground.

"Sorry," I said, figuring I needed an ally, even a pint-size one, and manners couldn't hurt.

I stood up and extended my hand and told him my name was Josiah and then I passed out.

When I came to I thought I'd somehow landed in the water below.

But that didn't make sense.

But I *was* wet.

And then I opened my eyes and saw the kid was pouring water on me.

I scrambled to my feet and the kid backed away.

"Please don't swear at me again, Mister."

"Sorry," I repeated. "How long was I out?"

"Just long enough for me to run to the well and get some water."

He had some left in a battered bucket and offered it to me and I drank it.

What was left of my brain started working again and I remembered that I was in enemy territory and dropped to one knee.

"They won't see you, Mister. They're all at church."

I regarded him for a moment. He was dressed in what probably passed for formal clothes in these mountains. His shirt was buttoned all the way to the top and he wore some sort of jacket with a collar that stood straight up. There was something odd about the clothes: something a bit off. I couldn't rightly say what.

"Why aren't you in church?" I asked.

"'Cause I can't stomach it no more."

"Won't they miss you?"

"Probably not. The kids sit in back and my parents get kinda hypnotized and wouldn't notice if I grew wings and flew out of there."

My instincts were demanding that I grab the kid by the lapels of his strange little jacket and demand an explanation of where Carmody was and who these people were and why somebody had shot me.

But my experience was telling me to slow down and build a relationship with my disaffected ally so I'd get the whole story. Something was eating him. When people get a chance to talk about what they're upset about they rarely hold back.

So I asked him what bothered him about church and he gave me the story.

And what a story it was.

The Reverend Ben Lobb had moved his supporters to the town about ten years ago.

My young friend, whose name was Christopher Provost, said he was the first baby born in Lobbtown.

And the church was called the First Church of Lobbtown.

The Reverend Lobb told them that there was an Apocalypse coming but his followers could survive if they followed his interpretations of the Bible – which meant living by his rules.

Those rules included turning over all money to the church, marrying according to the Reverend's wishes, and banishing heretics. A heretic was anyone who Lobb didn't like.

Christopher told me that while he didn't understand why, there was always a supply of recruits that more than kept up with the drain from banished heretics.

There were lots of people who were lost, Christopher told me, or afraid, or lonely.

The parishioners were real nice to them, at first, Christopher said, looking at the ground and tracing an arc in the dust with the toe of his boot.

"But pretty soon," he said, "they forgot what normal was."

Pretty perceptive kid. Lots of trouble in this world comes from people who forgot what normal was.

But in the past year or so there'd been trouble, he said. People from the network of towns in the mountain range had begun to kick about The Reverend and a few had begun to openly criticize him.

The Reverend told his followers that their own salvation was endangered by the heretics and he gave real clever reasons why, Christopher said, and backed up each part of the process with a quote from scripture.

Talk-and-quote, talk-and-quote, talk-and-quote, Christopher said, that's all the man did.

And people believed him and actually took paper and pencil to his services and *wrote that talk-and-quote stuff down.*

And when he told them to bring vengeance upon the heretics who were trying to muck up salvation they *did it.*

They're crazy, Christopher said.

They killed those people in the next town as a divine sacrifice, just like they were going to kill the tall guy I'd ridden in with.

I'd forgotten about Carmody. Somehow, it never occurred to me that he *could* be captured. But he'd given himself up, Christopher said, because he wouldn't shoot what with the women and kids around.

Lobb said Carmody was an agent of the devil and they would dispatch him at the service.

Christopher didn't want to see it.

The First Church of Lobbtown was two stories tall but there was no second floor; it was all open space, with no balcony. The windows were too high for me to look into but Christopher told me that the building was being painted and there was a ladder along one side and he'd set it up for me when he went back in.

I told him to set the ladder up but not to go back in the church.

He asked me why and I couldn't give him a good answer.

Christopher shrugged and left without saying anything more.

I gave him a minute and followed, and saw the ladder leading up to the lone rear window.

As a rule I don't like ladders, and this one was particularly unappealing because it and I had both deteriorated to a rickety state. It wobbled under my feet. And I was still seeing sparkles and got lightheaded when I moved too quickly.

But I forgot about my troubles when I poked my head slowly above the sill and saw what shape Carmody was in. He was on a slightly elevated platform and his wrists were lashed to two posts about eight feet apart. His arms were spread, crucifixion-style, and I couldn't help but marvel at his wingspread. He looked understandably glum but his eyes were alert and I could tell that the machinery behind them was cranking out escape plans.

There were 32 people in the church. Eleven men, five of them carrying visible sidearms, ten women, and eleven children of various ages.

I make it a habit to count exact numbers when I can. You never know when you're going

to need to know how many hostiles – or inno-
cents — are still out there in a fluid and unfolding situation. It doesn't take much longer to get
an exact number than it takes to make a guess.

One of the eleven men was Carmody and
the other was, I took it, the Reverend Lobb.

I could see how the little girl who'd escaped the slaughter could have mixed up Lobb
and our own befuddled minister. Both wore
beards, clerical collars, and jackets, though
Lobb's had that peculiar collar which I'm guessing is part of some uniform-like component of
the garb. Both had long hair and were balding
on top.

They resembled each other in every way
except one was a homicidal maniac while the
other, as far as I knew, was not.

And at the moment Lobb was holding a
knife; he held it aloft, showing it to the parishioners.

"A man who betrays and commits wick-
edness," Lobb said, using a broad and theatrical
cadence that sounded more like a comic actor
portraying a preacher in a stage play than a real
preacher, "must be brought to the gates and
killed."

There were mumbled murmurs of assent.

And then Carmody's backwoods tenor cut
through the burble.

"You only got half of that right." It came
out *ya only got half a that rot,* but it was reso-

nant and powerful as the pealing of a bell and everyone, including Lobb, was startled.

Lobb was a man clearly not accustomed to being interrupted, and as a result he didn't really know what to do.

He just stared.

"Deuteronomy Twelve says you can bring me to the gates and stone me," Carmody says, "though it looks like you're more likely to stick me than stone me. I can live with that screwed-up interpretation. But there's more to it later in the verse. You can kill me but only after you all 'enquired diligently,' and 'behold it to be true or certain.' You ain't done that."

There were a couple murmurs, more hushed than before.

"No enquiring or beholding as far as I can see," Carmody concluded.

"Nothing requires that I let an infidel spread the word of Satan," Lobb intoned.

"Bullshit," Carmody said, drawing it out – *bull sheeeeit* — out for effect.

He really had their attention now.

"Pardon my colorful language," Carmody said. "I ain't no cultured speaker. I just tell the truth as I see it."

Some parishioners exchanged glances and Lobb fiddled with the knife.

Carmody picked up the cadence.

"You want to shut me up? Well, they wanted to shut *Paul* up, too. And remember what the Lord told him in *Acts*? 'Do not be afraid, but go on speaking, and do not be silent because I am with you.'"

I couldn't tell for sure from my perch in the back but I gathered a few in the pews exchanged words with each other.

Suddenly, Carmody's voice filled the church.

I could feel the vibration in the window sill.

"You all are under the spell of a man who got at some of you to hack women and children to death," Carmody roared.

Lobb lost his ministerial composure.

"Shut the *fuck up*," he hissed.

Now there were heads turning, turning ninety degrees or farther. I hoped they wouldn't look too far behind them because if they spotted me I had no idea what I'd do. For the present, I was enjoying the show.

"I don't blame you folks," Carmody said, and the big mountain goat began making eye contact with the parishioners, one-by-one. "You came looking for comfort and guidance and you was an *easy mark* for a false prophet. But do you really believe the Lord wants you to live this way? Just because a man wears a collar don't mean nothing. He ain't talking for the Lord, he's talking for *hisself*."

Lobb parried.

"This man will soon be dead, and he should be. He spreads the word of Satan to attempt to make you defy me. Stay firm. Remember the word of Hebrews? 'Follow your leaders and submit to them, for they are keeping watch over your souls.'"

And Carmody counterpunched without missing a beat.

"And again he's telling you *half* the story. The rest of that verse, Hebrews 13:17, by the way, tells you that the leaders are supposed to be *held to account*. Anybody here find this man particularly accountable for his actions? Does he explain himself to *you*?"

"I have no need to explain," Lobb said, "as I speak for the Lord."

"You're a damn *criminal,*" Carmody said, and I could feel the window sill vibrating again. "You know half the Bible and twist it for your own purposes. You ain't the first to do that. Lots of people distort the word for evil intent. You *twist* the scripture. You're *untaught* and *unstable.* Them was *Peter's* words – how he described false prophets. Plain as day you're untaught when a guy like me who's lived his life lower than a snake's belly in a wagon rut out-scriptures you."

Lobb was stumped.

So he raised the knife, ceremonial-like, and made it plain he was going to get on with his business.

"And as far as unstable," Carmody screamed, "I picked up pieces of little kids on account of what you told people to do in your name. Not *God's* name. *Your* name."

Carmody, sensing that his stage-time was drawing to a close, surveyed the church.

"You people cannot follow him if God gives you a sign, right now," Carmody said. "That's black and white: 'You must abandon false prophets when you receive the sign from Josiah.'"

I wondered what sign from Josiah he anticipated.

Then I remembered that *I'm* Josiah.

I was still seeing sparkles in the corners of my eyes and it took me a minute.

Carmody had seen me. As I've noted, the man has remarkable eyes.

I guess Carmody made that part up about the sign because as I remember, which is not too clearly, King Josiah didn't do much except build a snazzy temple.

So...I needed to provide a sign, and I had just a few seconds to figure out what it would be.

I couldn't risk starting gunplay in a church full of children. Or endanger the men and women, for that matter; I had no idea who was guilty of what and although I expected most or all of the adults were complicit, I couldn't settle that here and now in a crossfire.

And although I might have no choice in the matter, because I couldn't let Carmody be disemboweled, I wasn't too keen about assassinating a minister, even a phony one, in front of his flock, even if that flock was some sort of an insane death cult.

"A *sign,*" Carmody said, with some impatience, "from Josiah, smiting the weapon from the hand of Satan."

He picked the oddest time to make jokes.

A few months ago I'd shot the revolver out of a gunfighter's hand. He'd gotten the drop on me and I'd managed to get off a panic shot, hoping, at best, it would go somewhere in his general direction.

Now, a bullet has to land somewhere – and in this case it hit the one square inch of the muzzle of his revolver and sent it spinning over his shoulder.

I didn't bother correcting the newspapers who characterized me as "the man with the lightning draw" who could shoot guns out of his opponents' hands. After all, what would I say...that I just as easily could have shot the ceiling or shot myself in the leg?

Carmody had needled me unmercifully, and I can't say that if the positions were reversed I wouldn't have done the same.

"Smiting *the weapon*," Carmody intoned again, loud, insistent.

Was he sensing my ambivalence about gunning down Lobb and instigating a running battle, and actually suggesting that I shoot the knife out of Lobb's hand?

I'm good with a gun, very good. Maybe not as good as the guys who stage the trick-shot shows and shoot coins out of the air, but in gunfights there are different meanings to the concept of good shots, which to someone in my line of work means shots that land where it counts.

"Smite," Carmody repeated.

Could I hit the hand holding the knife? Could I make a shot like that on trembling legs on a sagging ladder after getting my brain-pan scrambled after falling off a cliff?

"Smite, you dumb shit."

The knife pinwheeled away and the Reverend Ben Lobb stared with slack-jawed wonder at the neat, bleeding hole in the center of his palm.

When a gun goes off in a fairly small area it's not always easy to localize the sound and the parishioners looked in every direction except back, but they'd soon figure it out.

I wasn't sure why I didn't want to be seen other than staying anonymous would give me a couple more minutes to plan the next move.

I had to do something to keep the armed men in the crowd from thinking about going for their guns. And to keep Lobb occupied after the shock of getting shot in the hand wore off.

Carmody seemed to have the same idea. I also suspect he liked the attention and was beginning to enjoy himself.

"Do you all know the meaning of the Walls of Jericho?" Carmody asked, and heads swiveled forward.

"The walls were the obstacles to a *new life*. And sometimes obstacles have to tumble down."

With that he took a deep breath and pulled his bound hands inward, toward his chest.

It was like a circus strongman act.

I suspect that Carmody is actually stronger than most circus strongmen and probably a better performer, too.

The poles, about eight feet apart, began to creak, and then groan, and then pop.

Carmody's face was set in a mask of stony determination. He gritted his teeth and stared straight forward and pulled harder on the ropes.

Both pieces of wood snapped at the same time. They were support pillars; the roof sagged and the walls began to lean inward.

Carmody violently pulled the ropes loose from the broken pillars and grabbed Lobb by the lapels. I noticed that Carmody's hands were purple from lack of circulation and the ropes still bit into his wrists, which were bleeding.

He dragged Lobb off the stage and heaved him through the door.

The parishioners followed. The show had moved outdoors and they had no interest in staying inside a precariously leaning building.

So I climbed down the ladder and ran around to the church door.

About half the people were outside when I got there, knotted together. The others were bottlenecked up but they were making quick progress.

No one had pulled a gun yet.

Carmody was the last to leave. He'd untied his restraints and used them to bind Lobb's arms behind his back.

Now that everyone was standing still, we had a problem. The armed men were looking around and figuring out what to do.

I decided to give them a sign from Josiah.

"Until I sort this out," I said, "everyone here can consider themselves under arrest. Those of you who are armed, undo your gunbelts and let them drop to the ground."

No one moved, but they were thinking about it.

We had the type of standoff that usually does not end easily or end well.

"Drop them gunbelts!" Carmody intoned in his preacher voice.

And they obeyed, in unison, as cleanly as a troupe of dancers.

Carmody and I didn't talk much until we'd settled back in at the Spoon two nights later, me at the piano and Carmody in a chair next to me, the only seat left in the joint.

It was hopping.

As is his wont, Carmody dispensed with the glass after his first pint of whiskey and after opening the second one started sucking it straight out of the bottle.

Without a word, the little girl I'd found wandering the trails two days ago picked up Carmody's glass, placed it on a tray with some other dirties, and began washing them behind the bar.

Elmira, who was busy stocking the liquor, had put her to work. I wondered if that counted as exploitation or therapy or both.

Elmira looked at me, spread her arms, palms up in the universal "what else am I sup-posed to do" gesture, and gave me the eyebrow indicating it would be nice if I pitched in, too.

The graze across my back hurt and I still had a headache so I didn't feel the least bit guilty about not cleaning up the empties.

So I decided to talk with Carmody.

It wasn't that we'd been trying to avoid conversation over the last couple days. We'd been busy.

Arresting a whole town is a logistical nightmare.

Luckily I'd had some help. Carmody and I had to stay to keep order – the town had no jail so it was sort of a mass house-arrest situation — so I sent Christopher to Austin to fetch reinforcements. He'd offered to make the trip and of course I'd been skeptical about sending a ten-year-old boy on a four-hour night ride that involved some tricky mountain passes.

But Christopher said he knew the trails and when Carmody quizzed him about directions and roads he gave all the right answers. Carmody accompanied him for a mile or so to be sure he could handle the horse the way he said he could.

He could, and Carmody was back. None too soon for me.

Christopher had carried a letter. I found some paper and wrote to a state judge named Percival Weed explaining the situation. It took about five pages and entombed in cold print the scenario seemed improbable at best and fantastic at worst, but I knew Weed and my other friends in Austin would believe it because they would know I'm just not capable of making something like that up.

Weed and I had a set-to some months back – I had, in fact, thrown him in my cell for a few days– but he'd been a puppet in somebody else's game and after the whole mess had been straightened out Weed had not only been vindicated but emerged as something of a hero.

He owed me, in other words.

So I gave Christopher the letter, directions to the courthouse and Weed's residence, and my badge, which he could show to whoever asked in order to prove that the letter was for real and not the scribblings of an inmate in a mental hospital.

Ten constables ricocheted back by late afternoon the next day, men with big jaws and hard eyes and shiny brass buttons atop gleaming Morgan horses and boy was I glad to see them.

They took careful notes and called me "Sir" and conveyed hellos from people in Austin who knew me, and then they took the entire wretched problem off my hands, with the promise that I'd be called to testify at some point in the future.

Carmody pointed the neck of the bottle toward me. It was his way of offering to share.

I declined.

"You sure? I know you're squeamish about sharing a bottle because you think I've been eating squirrels but I ain't. Squirrels is just for emergencies. Besides, this whiskey of Elmira's would take paint off a barn so I think Louis Pasteur would guarantee this is free of them germs."

"Why the hell not?" I said, and took a pull.

Carmody did likewise and wiped his mouth with the back of his hand.

Then he handed me the empty bottle.

"You declared war on these things, I take it, so here's another for you to shoot at."

"You mean my little session of target practice," I said.

"You was out there blasting for two hours."

"Gun trouble. Checked out a problem with my Colt. Left it at the gunsmith's afterwards, which is why I'm wearing this overgrown mutant .44, which is so heavy it's giving me a backache."

Carmody nodded.

"And that leads me to an interesting subject," I said.

He gave me the eyebrow that says, *go ahead but don't assume I'm going to like it.*

"I knew you sometimes filled in as a chaplain," I said, "and that you'd been a lay preacher back in that place where you come from where a squirrel and a case of whiskey's called a thirteen-course dinner. But what I saw you do back in that hellhole showed more than a casual acquaintance with the matter at hand."

"Showed I am a good actor, that's all, especially when somebody's fixing to fillet me like a catfish and I need to keep stalling while my hero rescuer diddles around trying to figure out what to do."

Carmody seemed suddenly serious and, improbably, sober.

"Funny thing about religion," he said. "You knew that guy was nothing but a thug and a phony and that whole church was just a sham for him to shepherd a bunch of deviants. But you couldn't bring yourself to shoot him. I've seen you shoot people 'cause you thought they was *looking* at you funny, but you had trouble pulling the trigger on that guy on account he was wearing a collar."

"Yes," I said. There was nothing more to add. He was right.

"And that's the way it s*hould* be," Carmody said, surprising me. "Gotta have borders. Gotta give some institutions the benefit of the doubt, because even though they ain't perfect and sometimes go one-hundred-percent haywire, they're symbols of civilization."

"Sounds good to me," I said.

"Of *course* it sounds good to you. You said it near a year ago when that bank robber you was chasing hid out in a church and you waited for him to come out. I repeated it back to you 'cause it does make some sense but mostly because I know how much you respond to the sound of your own talking."

I laughed in spite of myself.

"I don't pretend to have all the answers," I said. "In fact, the older I get the more I realize what I don't know."

"And you don't know about religion?" he said. "After the shit you've seen, you still hold out hope that there's really heaven, mercy, and miracles?"

"In a former life, I told students that it's good to be a skeptic, but a true skeptic doesn't necessarily disbelieve what can't be disproven."

"That is a very heavy load of thought for me to handle," Carmody said. "Let me go across the street to the stable to retrieve a tool they keep handy to shovel up such stuff."

I was getting tired of talking in circles.

"What happened to your arm?" I said.

He pretended not to understand.

"What happened to your arm?" I repeated.

"It's just bizarre that a stump-jumper like me has to lecture a fancy officer and professor about science but I *did* see the doctor in Head Horse Hill and he said things like that just *happen*. You get a condition where the mind sort of shuts down talking to an injured part of the body, 'specially when moving it hurts so much."

I gave him an eyebrow this time.

"Times of dire emergency, though –
them's the doctor's words, *dire emergency* —
like when you're about to be opened up like a
trout and your partner's diddling with himself,
and some psycho wearing a collar is pissing all
over an institution I don't necessarily believe in
but respect, you can work up a huge surge of
strength. Ladies lift tipped over stagecoaches
off their kids, stuff like that. In my case, the doc
says, that's what happened and it brought that
arm back to life. It still hurts, but it works."

"You tore down a *fucking building*," I
said.

Carmody turned to me and winked.

"Just between us," he said, "back home I
put up a lot of structures and I knew enough to
nail supporting beams into a cross member, not
right into the roof like those dickheads did
when they built that shitbox."

"Fair enough," I admitted. "The arm's not
divine intervention, and neither was the
strength to pull the building down and scare the
shit out of all those people who figured you
must be the new Messiah. But what about the
shot that took the knife out of Lobb's hand?"

He seemed surprised.

"Wasn't no miracle. Miracle was that I
figured out how you could get your head out of
your ass in time to shoot, but what are we talking, sixty feet at the most? Easy shot for you."

"I took a bath this morning," I said.

"And we are all appreciative of that. So?"

"I put my gun on the table and when I got down into the tub I was looking at an angle and could see it was bent. I not only dropped the fucking thing about 20 feet when I fell off that cliff but I also fell down and landed on it."

"I am hopeful that there is a point here," Carmody said.

"The point is that this morning I took it out and test-fired it. Probably a hundred shots. The barrel's bent so much that at fifty-five feet it shoots two feet to the left."

Carmody stared straight ahead.

"The window and where you were tied up is fifty-five feet. I can tell distance to the inch. You know that."

No reaction.

"Two feet left would have been dead center of your chest."

Some cowhands came in through the batwings and there was laughter and loud talk.

"Maybe my aim was off," I said, "because I scrambled my brains in the fall and was bleeding from the graze on my back and was standing on a ladder that wasn't built much better than that church. So maybe it was just because I was so beat up that I aimed two feet in the wrong direction."

"Maybe," he said, and took a long pull on the bottle.

"Did you get the gun straightened out?" he asked when he was finished.

"No, the smith can't get to it until tomorrow afternoon. And straightening a barrel's not easy, so he's not sure it can be fixed."

Carmody stood up, told me he'd be right back, and asked if I would cowpoke up something cheerful on the piano.

He returned in a moment.

"Not that I don't believe you, but I'm a good skeptic, too. Mind if we get that gun back from the smith in the morning and I give it a try?"

"Not at all," I said.

He placed a new bottle of whiskey on top of the piano.

"Got us an extra target," he said, and he sat back and listened to the music.

THE END

FURY — ON THE FAR HORIZON

A HAWKE & CARMODY WESTERN SHORT STORY

CARL DANE

RAGING BULL PUBLISHING

I recognized her, of course.

After all, during the war I'd slept with her once and shot her twice. You tend not to forget things like that, even after more than a decade.

I could tell she remembered me, too, but she doused the flicker of recognition as quickly as it had ignited, and continued with her dance, not missing one noisy beat. She'd been a spy and probably a killer, although the only person I definitely knew she'd tried to kill had been me, so she wasn't about to be thrown too far off-balance by a face from the past.

She'd called herself Salona Pixley then, and for all I knew that was her real name. Unless there's some reason why your real name would get you into trouble, it's usually best to use it because the fewer lies you have to tell, the easier it is to keep track of them.

During the time when our orbits intersected I'd been a Union officer working undercover in assignments I wasn't supposed to talk about. I wondered if the prohibition still applied, and who would enforce it if it did.

I abandoned that line of thought because it's not something I wanted to share with the occupants of my current world, anyway.

Salona never knew me by my real name. I'd been a real Union officer when not on special assignment involving "targeted operations," as we called it, and there was always a chance somebody could trace me back on a roster, so I called myself Josiah Hatch. Before that I'd been Josiah Hosmer, and for a while after I was Josiah Hilton.

I was never one to carry stuff with monograms or anything like that, but using your real initials can help keep you from getting tripped up. Using your real first name ensures you'll remember to answer when spoken to.

When your life depends on the convincing cadence of every lie, you need all the advantages you can muster.

For the record, my real name is Josiah Hawke, and today I'm the town marshal in Shadow Valley, a backward little berg in the Texas Hill Country that nevertheless is not without its charms, which include my girlfriend Elmira Adler. Elmira owns a bar and bordello called the Silver Spoon, as well as the stage where Salona Pixley was dancing.

About a year ago Elmira bought out the millenary shop next door to the Spoon, knocked it down, and built this combination theater, meeting hall, and church. It seemed an odd mixture of ventures to me at the time, but Elmira has a good head for business and a good heart for the community. She knows that churches are essential for towns like ours – remote and occasionally violent outposts – to grow and prosper.

But Elmira astutely observed that a church usually sits empty six-and-a-half days a week, and usually half-empty the remaining fraction of the time, and she designed the space to double as a theater.

She'd managed to book some halfway-decent shows and theater companies that travel in these parts, and while Shadow Valley isn't exactly on the way to or from anything, it does sit about halfway between Austin and San Antonio so we weren't in the opposite direction of civilization, either.

And that is what led me to the most improbable scenario of attending a traveling show in a theater that doubles as a church and shares a wall, as well as common ownership, with a whorehouse – all while watching a woman who'd set me up for death a dozen years ago stomp her feet to music.

Elmira was wedged to my right. The seating was pew-style, punishingly tight and narrow. I tried to talk her out of such compact accommodations on humanitarian grounds, but she'd insisted, in her unique syntax, that it was "necessarily necessary" to maximize return on investment by fitting in as many butts as possible.

We were squeezed in the middle of the fourth row – a silly position as I would have to extricate myself during the show both to play piano and patrol the bar next door – but Elmira had heard someone say that fourth row center was the best seat in the house and she insisted on occupying it, even if it did cost me the blood flow to my legs.

I'm not crazy about tight quarters, but on the bright side, having Elmira squashed up against me felt wonderful.

My deputy, Tom Carmody, was seated to my left, also pressed tight against me, and it felt just awful. Carmody is about six-five, maybe a little taller. Due to the constraints of geometry, there was no way his legs could fit in a normal seated position while stuffed into the pew, so one knee was up on the back of the pew in front of us and the other was jammed into my thigh. Carmody seemed to somehow be constructed entirely of knees and elbows and other sharp, incessantly moving, protrusions.

Carmody also likes to lecture me while emphasizing his endless chatter by pointing with an index finger that's as long and gnarly as a tree branch. In our enforced close quarters he also found it necessary to jab it into my shoulder as he talked.

"I never seen nobody get so light and high in the air," he said, punctuating the sentence with two thrusts.

It came out *ah niver seen nobody git so lahtt 'n hahh in the arrrrhh.* He was from the mountains of Eastern Tennessee, and while he had lately taken to wearing vested suits and crisp bowlers, he somehow made all his expensive haberdashery look like overalls and a straw hat.

"What she's doing is called Lancashire clog dancing," Carmody said, pointing that finger at the stage, poking me in the shoulder with it, and then pointing back at the stage just in case I somehow had missed the connection. For reasons unknown to me, Carmody – who grew up eating squirrels in mountains so strange and remote that even non-native squirrels shunned the vicinity – had somehow amassed an encyclopedic knowledge of music.

I play piano, a vestige of an earlier, civilized life before the war, and I can rarely stump him on a piece of music, new or classical. I play an old but serviceable upright nights at the Spoon, and when I run out of current repertoire, all of which Carmody has somehow not only heard but memorized, I slip in some Bach or Mozart. If I give it a strong beat, a process Carmody calls "cowpoking it up," nobody knows the difference.

Except for Carmody, who can identify the composer, title, movement, and any repeats or key changes I might forget.

"Lancashire's in *England*," Carmody said, warming to his lecture. "That's in *Europe*."

"I've heard that," I assured him.

"They got lot of mills there, and because the floors is always wet the workers wear shoes with wood soles. They got the idea to dance with them and clickety-clack the rhythms. Hard to believe she can stand there all straight and proper and pound out them beats like a Gatling gun."

Carmody was right about Salona. She appeared to float an inch off the ground, her upper body motionless as an icicle, but her feet a graceful blur. The thick shoes industriously hammered out an intricate rhythm as she danced to an accompaniment provided by a tiny older man seated next to her, sawing on a violin.

"Cloggers is real popular in these traveling shows," Carmody said, rearranging his various limbs and managing to dig an elbow into my ribs.

"Dancing is perfect for the *dumb act*," he said. "The dumb act means it ain't got no words. Don't mean it's *stupid* dumb. It's a good opener when people is still coming in and the audience keeps talking."

"Like now," I said, hoping he'd get the hint.

"Yep," Carmody said, and kept talking. "The way it usually works is that after the dumb act, you get them to settle down with some singing, something sentimental, follow with something serious like a Bible reading, and then warm them up with some comedy or a minstrel act. Then they're ready for the drama."

Up on stage Salona did a pirouette, feet crossing and uncrossing, toes pointed in and then out, but with her hands hanging at her side and her body perfectly vertical. When she rotated back to the audience, her eyes held mine for another moment. She didn't want to look, I don't think, but she couldn't help herself. Kind of like when you suspect there is a spider on your shoulder but you really don't want to confront the reality so you steal a couple quick glances.

"Amazing they can flail away like that down below but keep like a statue up above," Carmody said. "Story goes that they wasn't supposed to have no fun in England and Ireland," he continued, "so they learned how to do the steps with their bodies all stiff-and-straight-like, so nobody looking in the window could tell they was dancing. That's why they dance like they got ramrods up their butts."

Carmody has a unique way of putting things.

He was making ready to prod me again when I felt Elmira twist herself a little in my direction. I thought about putting my arm around her but she'd pinned my elbow against my side, where it was in the process of falling asleep. But on the positive side she certainly smelled nice, and with her practically on top of me and my arm going numb I wouldn't be able to draw my weapon, a tantalizing prospect because Carmody's finger was approaching my shoulder again.

"Don't know if I believe that story, however," he said, prodding me. "If they was trying to be sneaky, why would they be stomping around like that?"

It was an interesting point, and I was going to reply, but I lost the thread of the conversation when Salona stole another furtive glance at me.

She was as beautiful as the last time I'd seen her, and didn't look much over thirty, although she had to be by now. She had shoulder-length dark hair, intense brown eyes, and was very thin. Not sick-thin; more like racehorse-thin. I guess you stay in good shape stomping around all the time.

Carmody, who misses nothing in life except my occasional homicidal exasperation with him, noticed that Salona was looking at me but said nothing. He could sense that now was not the time or place to bring it up, and his measured judgment in the professional aspects of our lives was one reason why I valued him enough to keep him on the payroll and not to shoot him. That and the fact that he'd saved my life more than I'd saved his.

Elmira stirred again and I thought I could feel her eyes on me, though I didn't think it likely that she'd noticed Salona's glances. Don't get me wrong: Elmira is indeed the jealous type, constantly envisioning fantastic – though admittedly flattering — scenarios in which every woman I encounter is surreptitiously plotting to seduce me.

But she does that by rote and on reflex, assuming the worst every time I have an interaction with another woman involving one of us saying "hello" or something equally sinister.

In terms of picking up nuance, though, Elmira is generally blind and oblivious to her surroundings, so I wasn't worried about her catching on to Solana's sidelong and surreptitious sneak-peeks.

Last month, Carmody and I painted the stark white walls of the bar blue. Carmody had read somewhere that insane asylums had adopted that color to calm the inmates and figured that because we were dealing with essentially the same type of clientele it was worth a try, so we got up early and figured we'd surprise Elmira when she came down from her room upstairs.

She *didn't notice.*

Later than night one of the waitresses couldn't stand it any longer and asked Elmira how it was possible that she did not notice that the walls were now blue.

"What color *were* they?" Elmira had asked.

So I wasn't expecting a problem when I felt her tap my on the shoulder. Everybody was communicating with index fingers tonight. I was squeezed in so tightly that I had to work up some momentum to spin and twist toward her.

Her head was facing front but her eyeballs were cut toward me, cranked so far into the corners of the sockets that it must have actually *hurt* to do that.

I've always described her eyes as being clear and blue as a mountain lake.

They were still clear and blue but at the moment looked more like a frozen mountain like. Or maybe an iceberg.

She spit out the beginnings and bit off the ends of each of the words she spoke next.

"I take it," she said, "that you know that...that *clog-hopper*."

For a second I marveled at how she had mutated a cowboy insult for a farmer who trod clods of dirt into a slur that made, well, no sense whatsoever.

And then my survival instincts kicked in.

In an instant I had a cover story all framed out in my mind, something about another town where I'd been lawing – of course, I couldn't be expected to remember which one – and I thought I recognized Salona as one of a troupe of actors I'd had to evict from a hotel for nonpayment of a bill.

That's how she remembers me, I rehearsed in my mind.

It was a perfect cover, specific enough to be believable, general enough to be deniable if I got caught with an error in the details, and perfectly plausible. I'd had to shoo plenty of deadbeat show people out of hotels over the years, though they were generally not a threat to anyone's safety so I would usually work out alternative accommodations if it was cold or late at night.

I'd mentioned things like that to Elmira before, so I had the perfect story.

I felt a mild rush of satisfaction.

And then a flash of anger.

It wasn't 1964, I reminded myself. I wasn't behind enemy lines, my life didn't depend on covering my tracks, and there was *no damned reason* to lie. What I'd done with Salona and *to* Salona happened years before I met Elmira, and she had no justification for her jealously and I had no earthly need to lie.

For a second or two I wondered why my mind had started working that way – concocting cover stories. The unexpected reappearance of Salona Pixley had, I guess, dragged me back to another a time. A time of plots and lies, a time when she'd lured me into bed to keep me off the trail of my target. A time when I'd been younger, and apparently appeared more gullible, although a few hours later she'd learned – the hard way – that I wasn't.

Damn her, I thought. She'd turned me back into Josiah Hatch. Or Hosmer, or Hilton, or whoever I'd been.

So I revived my present-moment self and looked Elmira directly in her painfully slanting eyes and told her the truth.

The dance act was ending and Salona was taking her bows and people were applauding, so it was pretty noisy when I explained the situation. It apparently wasn't easy for Elmira to hear, and it addition to that, she probably had a headache from cranking her eyes so far to the left.

So I suppose it was partially my fault. I should have expected that she'd get the story mixed up.

And I shouldn't have told her right when the act was ending because the applause was dying down when Elmira pointed at Salona and *shouted*.

"You shot that girl down and *then had sex with her?*"

I started to explain that she had the order reversed but realized that the place was dead silent and every eye was on me and it was none of their damn business anyway.

Besides, I had a job to do.

I had to play piano for the next act.

Elmira had volunteered me to accompany the singer and of course had forgotten to tell me until we'd been seated. I'd never met the singer nor seen the sheet music, but the ballads sung in these shows are generally pretty straightforward so I didn't anticipate much of a challenge.

I climbed over a half-row of audience members, all fully equipped with pointy elbows, and then moved to the piano as quickly as I could.

I was anxious to start playing as loudly as possible because Carmody's voice travels like a rifle shot and as I flipped open the sheet music he was earnestly explaining to Elmira that he was *almost certain* that I'd said I'd slept with the clog-hopper *before* I'd shot her.

"The other way don't make no sense at all," he implored, in a whisper that you could have heard in Austin. "I mean not to a *normal* person."

Out of habit, I took a look at the spectators over the top of the upright, which Carmody and I had wheeled over from the saloon. It was angled so I could see the stage and the audience.

I noticed that they were looking at me like I was some exotic predatory zoo specimen.

I busied myself with the sheet music and ad-libbed some introductory chords using the basic melody line. Loudly. Anything to drown out Carmody's earnest defense of my mating habits.

I saw the man I presumed to be the singer bustle on stage. He hadn't expected me to start playing so soon, and cut me a hard glance before turning to the audience and smiling.

He was a medium-short, portly man with a graying black beard and coal-hard eyes.

Then he gave a perfunctory nod, I presume to let me know I could start the music for real.

And so I turned back into Josiah Hatch and nodded back and did not betray anything.

Not a damn thing.

He didn't recognize me.

There was to reason he should have. He couldn't have seen me the day he made his escape. I'd been more than a thousand feet away and viewing him through an Amidon telescope bolted onto a Sharps rifle, a big-bore breech-loader, and he'd been in my cross-hairs the last time I saw him.

The idea of a telescopic sight sounds good in theory but in the real world it's a lot more complicated than you might suspect. There are problems of adjusting for windage and elevation and focus. Various units on the North and South had tried them out but in general the gadgets just gave you a better view of what you've missed.

Still, the scouts had found me an elevated position from which to fire and I'd been ordered to use the contraption, so I tried.

I'd missed, though I don't think it was entirely my fault. I think he somehow felt the sights on him; some people in the line of fire develop than sense, somehow, even though I can't explain it. He'd hit the ground and rolled, showing an agility that surprised me because he wasn't exactly thin back then, either.

And then he darted into a stand of pines and was gone.

I was almost sure of it. The face in the crosshairs thirteen years ago was the same one that was now warbling a syrupy song titled *Silver Threads Among the Gold,* a sentimental piece about love and growing old. Cowhands, a lot of whom would just as soon shoot you as say hello, get all misty-eyed at that stuff. That and any song with the word "mother" in it.

I studied him closely as he sang in a powerful baritone. It was an opportunity you're not always afforded – to look closely at a man's features. It draws attention in everyday life, but here I could stare all I want.

I'd only seen him once through the lens, and I'd identified him that day because he matched the description I'd been given and as far as I knew, no one matching that description would be running for his life from Union troops.

I have a good memory for faces. There were the same cold eyes, long earlobes, and odd eyebrows with a peak, like chevrons. With men, anyway, the eyebrows are a feature that doesn't change with much with age and aren't typically disguised. Men trying to do the chameleon bit grow beards or shave them off, gain or lose weight, or maybe even dye their hair. But they forget about eyebrows and can't really do much about ears, except cover them up with hair, if they have enough.

I didn't have to look at the music much as I ran an inventory of his features. I'd heard the tune before, and the accompaniment was just the top line of the melody with the right hand and some standard arpeggios with the left. The main tune alternated with two choruses.

After the right kind of training you can take one glance at the overall structure and figure out what's going to happen in the next few moves.

That principle applies to music and killing, and I'd been pretty well trained in both.

We finished the piece on a maudlin line, *life is fading fast away,* and the last chord was meant to be melancholy and haunting. I decided to play with the damper pedal a little, which allows you to fade the sound slowly away if you're good at the technique, and I made the last chord die perfectly.

And as the sound ebbed, I wondered if I would engineer a similar fate for Commandant Joseph Lefler, if indeed that was the rotund man now taking his third bow and sweeping a hand in my direction, calling for a round of applause for the accompanist. His gracious gesture contrasted oddly with those obsidian eyes that still stared right through me.

I nodded to him and then to the audience, who stopped clapping like a faucet was shut off as soon as I stood up. I clambered back to my seat, enduring some cold stares, including Elmira's, but I didn't notice much because my mind was elsewhere – a prison camp at Courter Crossing, Georgia, to be precise – and the next few moves were unfolding in my head, almost like some steam engine had taken control of my brain.

The mean-eyed round man stayed on stage and continued with a short Bible reading, which was standard fare for these types of traveling shows. He spoke about Jesus forgiving his betrayers. Along with saccharine songs about undying love, Bible verses are can't-miss cowhand and drifter fare. To a man, they sat placidly, most with their hands in the laps.

The next act was comedy of sorts, and the audience was not so demure. I didn't listen closely enough to tell if the act was funny or not, though there were some critics in the rear who apparently didn't think so and expressed their disdain by standing up and throwing some black potatoes, which the comic dodged with practiced skill. I guess throwing-and-dodging is an expected part of the experience as it seems to happen at every show I'd ever seen out West. You'd think the comics would wise up and stick to Bible verses for the sake of their own safety.

But I was in no mood for flying potatoes nor for the potential of other objects – maybe some of them made out of lead — to start to fly if things got more rowdy. Keeping order, in fact, was one reason why I and Carmody were here and not next door. Elmira wanted nothing to go wrong with her new ventures, and while I was not happy about both Carmody and I shirking our baby-sitting duties at the Spoon, it was still early by bar standards.

Serious mayhem next door probably wouldn't begin in earnest for an hour or so.

I managed to un-wedge myself enough to half-stand, turn, and glare at the potato-tossers, who sat down in unison.

I have a menacing glare – I practice, because it's an essential part of my job – but it had never worked this well before. Maybe being reviled as the marshal who hunted down his sexual conquests like quail had some advantages.

So I sat back down. Elmira wasn't looking at me, I noticed. Not even sideways. She stared stonily, straight ahead at the next act, which consisted of the little man who played fiddle for Salona's dance delivering a speech from Shakespeare.

You wouldn't think Shakespeare would work with our type of clientele, but it was popular fare for traveling shows throughout the West. When you come right down to it, it really wasn't the type of stuff written for high society in the first place; Shakespeare's audiences probably were of a similar social class for the era, although they probably didn't carry potatoes or guns.

The little fellow filled the hall with his outsized voice as he acted out Antony's oration over Caesar's body.

It went over well. He was a good actor and it's a damn clever bit of writing, something that even the drifters can identify with. Antony is angry that Brutus and his friends killed Caesar and so he gets up at Caesar's funeral and pretends to be going along with it, saying one thing but meaning another. He tricks the crowd into turning against Brutus.

The little actor with the big voice not only took the inevitable involvement of the audience in good stride but made them part of the act. After he'd opened with, *"Friends, Romans, Countrymen..."* he waited a beat for a handful of rowdies – including Carmody, as it happened – to finish: *"Lend me your ears."*

And so it went as the little man's Antony made his case point-by-point, assuring the funeral-goers that Brutus must have had a damn good reason for plotting against Caesar even if

Antony couldn't figure out what it was, and even though the evidence showed just the opposite.

Near the end of the soliloquy the crowd becomes outraged, turns on Brutus, and riots.

The dialogue for the crowd was provided by cast and crew members from offstage. And then the audience chimed in, too.

"We'll burn the house of Brutus!" shouted a voice backstage.

"Seek the conspirators!" yelled another.

"Goddamn *right!*" added the old man who swept up at the stables, seated in the front row of the audience.

"String 'em up!" implored the blacksmith, normally among the most peaceable of men.

Shakespeare could really stir people into a good outrage.

I was enjoying the show, and for a minute I marveled at how this small crew somehow managed to create distant rumblings of scuffling, thuds and angry shouts. Then I realized that the adjoining wall – on the other side of the bar — was shaking and occasionally *bulging* as, presumably, various bodies were thrown into it.

There was a *real* riot going on next door.

Such events were not entirely unexpected at the Spoon, although it was a little early in the evening for fisticuffs. Then again, it was cattle drive season and there were various crews in town and those groups did not exactly share a tradition of peaceful coexistence.

I told Elmira I had to go next door to quiet the natives and she cut her eyeballs toward me again and nodded in a curt sort of way.

Carmody was wrapped up in the show, so I had to poke him hard with my index finger to get his attention. I enjoyed doing that.

"Trouble next door," I said, and poked him again.

As he began to pry himself off the bench I had a notion, a vague thought.

"Don't let them notice you're tall," I said. "And turn your face away from the actors when you leave."

Most people would have barraged me with a hundred questions – questions I couldn't answer because I didn't completely know why I had issued those instructions – but Carmody was a professional. He realized that despite my other eccentricities I probably had a good reason for asking, even if it was only a hunch I couldn't explain. We'd been down that road many times.

So he jammed his hat low and kept hunched over as he bulled his way down the pew.

No one noticed Carmody much, anyway, because the little actor had the audience at a high fever.

As we picked our way through the spectators who blocked our exit, Carmody apparently forgot himself, turned slightly, and yelled, *"pluck down benches!"*

"Damn it," I said.

"Sorry," he said. "I got carried away."

"I never knew what that line meant, anyway," I admitted, for lack of anything better to say as we continued elbowing toward the door. "What did they want with benches, anyway?"

"Them benches was made out of wood. They was gonna burn them."

"How do you *know* this stuff?" I asked, for possibly the thousandth time, with no more hope of getting a real answer than the previous 999 times I'd asked.

"I ain't no dummy," Carmody said, and left it at that.

We hit the batwing doors to the Spoon a few seconds later. We didn't plan anything out in advance. We knew this particular routine as well as Salona knew the steps in her clog dance.

I threw back the left batwing door with an outstretched arm and stood to the side. Hearing no shots and seeing no bullets or bottles coming in my direction, I entered the room and cut diagonally to the right, the opposite way a man would normally move when entering a room. Carmody did the same pattern in reverse.

Neither of us drew our weapons before we entered. It's a calculated risk, to be sure, but barging into a room with guns drawn tends to further confuse and inflame the situation. Scared and angry people might take you for a member of the opposite team and play it safe by killing you first and sorting out your allegiance after the fact.

I was hoping to keep everybody's guns in their holsters.

But I saw that it was too late for that.

A lean man with high cheekbones and narrow, slanting eyes was pointing a big Colt at a shorter man who wore a buckskin jacket that was drawn tight around his bulging middle.

The guy with the cheekbones wore a glossy black leather vest and a crisp beaver bowler and possessed the broad face, small nose, and narrow cast to his eyes that I'd come to associate with the Slavs I'd met in mining country. He looked like a miner, in fact, despite the fancy clothes. If I had to guess, I'd peg him as a coal-gopher who'd fought his way out of one of those hardscrabble towns in Pennsylvania or thereabouts and would do absolutely anything to keep from going back.

The doughy, disheveled man in the dirty buckskins looked exactly like a doughy, disheveled man in dirty buckskins. One of thousands of anonymous and interchangeable down-and-outers who scrambled around cattle country for odd jobs and their next meal. I took him for a wrangler or somebody on the low end of the totem pole in the cattle drives. He wasn't a tough guy, I could tell. He was breathing hard, his nose was bleeding, and the side of his face was already swelling, presumably from a beating that Cheekbones had just laid on him.

Buckskin wasn't much of a draw, either. The tip of his barrel hadn't yet cleared the holster and he was frozen in position – afraid to pointlessly and suicidally resume his motion, but equally afraid to abandon it and abandon any pretense of defense.

The hammer on the tall man's Colt was fully drawn and I could see the flattening of the flesh around his trigger finger as he exerted maybe half of the four pounds of pull needed to fire.

I was ten feet away and didn't have any other option at the moment other than to try to talk them out of it.

I walked toward them slowly and said, in a soft voice, that I was the marshal and would appreciate it if they would slowly lower their guns.

Carmody announced his presence and read from roughly the same script, and began working his way to a point directly opposite where I stood. There's no perfect position for a confrontation like that, but at least we'd be out of the gunmen's immediate line of fire.

Buckskin, in a dithering panic, turned to look at me, and started to talk.

I told him to hold still, but it was too late. In the process of twisting toward me he'd absently cleared his gun from the holder.

It wasn't exactly what you'd call a draw. Then again, it wasn't like putting your gun down, either.

It was, in the final analysis, a good excuse for Cheekbones to fire.

Time slows down in moments like that. I saw one more tiny movement of the hammer on the big Colt; even when that type of revolver is fully cocked the trigger pull still brings the hammer back a fraction of an inch.

I saw Carmody moving toward Cheekbones as I advanced on Buckskin.

But there was nothing either of us could do as the hammer fell.

And then there was an astonishingly loud noise.

It was, in the dead silence of the room, the loudest click I'd ever heard.

And then there was another click. And then silence, as the mechanism froze.

When it became obvious that his gun wasn't going to fire, Cheekbones began to raise his hands in the universal "I didn't mean it" gesture.

I told Buckskin to drop his weapon and kept moving toward him.

Buckskin had one of those rubbery faces that molded itself into exaggerated, clown-like expressions as quickly as thoughts could cross his mind, which wasn't really that rapid of a process, but in the second or two it took me to cross the room I could see his expression change from confusion to rage – rage undoubtedly built up during the thousand times in his life this buttery little man had been pushed around.

Buckskin ignored me and fired.

I lunged for the gun and snagged it with my left hand. Most of my grip was on the barrel, which of course burned hell out of my palm. I cursed and brought the edge of my right hand down hard on the top of Buckskin's forearm, an inch from the elbow where there's a bundle of nerves that control the hand.

My aim was good because he let go immediately and I took control of the gun.

Carmody drew his revolver and bellowed for everyone to raise their hands.

The man has one hell of a set of lungs.

I damn near raised *my* hands.

It all happened so quickly that Cheekbones hadn't even hit the ground yet. He was collapsing straight down limb-by-limb, like a marionette when you release the strings. His hand was at center of his chest and he draw it away to gape at it, saw that it was painted in blood, and then the light left his eyes.

The confrontation was ended, I had Buckskin's gun, and then the inevitable happened.

Some idiot reached for a weapon.

It was another hard-looking man who'd been standing near Cheekbones, presumably one of his friends and also presumably looking for revenge on Buckskin. He was tall and muscular and wore a thin mustache that complemented his cold, practiced expression of malice. He looked a little like the guy who'd just been shot, enough to be his brother. Maybe he was.

He pulled so fluidly that I knew he was no stranger to gunplay.

Well, neither was I.

I put a round in the center of his forehead before he could get off a shot, and it was over.

Carmody and I ushered everybody out and closed up the Spoon for the night. You hate to do that on a big night but there was a fully equipped competitor, The Full Moon, down the street and the staff there would be more than happy to absorb the overflow.

Trouble in a bar usually begets nothing but more trouble. One of the friends of the two dead men – and he seemed to have a lot of friends in the bar — had backed out of the place snarling, *"We'll be back and you're in big trouble."*

I employed my finely honed detective instincts and concluded that I was going to be in big trouble, but that was sometime in the future. There was nothing I could do about it now, not with a room full of them, and I was happy to see them leave.

The round little man in the buckskins told me his name was Rufus Messenger, and he was a wrangler with an outfit headed to Kansas.

Messenger said that Cheekbones and the guy I'd killed were rustlers. I'd figured that out already, just from looking at them. There's a breed of rustler that indeed moves cattle from Point A to Point B but also steals them from every other stop along the alphabet, and is not averse to a little strong-arm robbery along the way, and the dead men fit the bill.

Carmody and I followed a protocol I'd invented more than a year ago: We rolled the dead bodies in blankets and kept them in the corner of the office for two days to see if anybody claimed them or otherwise showed interest. Then we'd bury them in our sorry little cemetery on a hill just outside of town.

We don't have an undertaker. Like most small settlements in our isolated region, which Carmody calls "The Backside of Beyond," we relied on undertakers, preachers, judges, doctors and the like who rode circuits and stopped at regular intervals. But our undertaker had died a couple years ago and we never could find a replacement, so it became incumbent on me to dispose of the dead bodies.

As I produced most of the supply, that only seemed fair.

Actually, Carmody routinely did the shovel-work. He was remarkably facile in the skills of grave-digging and though he never directly told me as much, I knew it was a skill he'd picked up during the war.

Carmody had been a sergeant with Tennessee's First Regiment Volunteer Infantry, a rugged Union outfit in a divided state that saw more bloodshed on its soil than anywhere else except Virginia.

I had been an officer, a misdeed for which Carmody has never forgiven me. But I hadn't been the braid-and-sword type of soldier. My unit, from southern Illinois, specialized in what the army called "special tactics." The people upon whom we perpetrated our special tactics called them "dirty tricks." And there was a brief period where I engaged in what my commander called "targeted operations."

It was a time I'd never told Carmody or Elmira about, but the reappearance of Salona Pixley meant, among other things, that I'd have to.

And in the process, I'd have to come up with a nice way of explaining what *targeted operations* really meant.

I heard Carmody and Elmira talking in the back room of the Spoon when I returned from locking Messenger in a cell for the night. I hadn't decided what to charge him with. I can't blame him for wanting to kill a man who'd beaten him up and drawn on him, but it was clear that Cheekbones was raising his hands and there was no need to fire.

In another life, long ago and before the war, I'd taught philosophy in a small Illinois college, and these sorts of issues would figure prominently in what I realize now was unfailingly remote and detached classroom discussion. Whether to charge a man with murder when he'd killed someone who not only drew on him but pulled the trigger on a misfiring gun would have been an intriguing scenario.

Now it was nothing but an administrative pain in my ass. I didn't blame Messenger for wanting to do what he did; from our brief conversation it became plain to me that he'd been pretty much a professional victim all his life, and who can blame a man for wanting to win a battle, just once. But as a practical matter a lawman can't let someone gun down another man who has his hands in the air. It sets a bad precedent.

As I opened the door to Elmira's back office, I decided the matter of what to do with Messenger could wait. That's what they make mornings for.

Carmody was so wrapped up in his monologue that he didn't hear me turn the knob.

"We both realize that Josiah ain't exactly the purtiest man in the world," Carmody said, still trying to placate Elmira, "but I do believe he can manage to, well, *cultivate* a relationship with a woman without having to drop her with a bullet first."

Elmira was about to answer when she saw me and forcefully crafted her expression into stone.

Carmody cleared his throat and took a sudden interest in the ceiling.

"There's something I need to tell both of you," I said, sitting down and taking my time about it.

"Do you really *think so*?" Elmira asked.

"I'm not interested in bickering about this," I said. My voice held an edge that I didn't intend, but I had to go on and I needed to get it over with. "We've got some problems and I have some things to tell you that you're not going to like to hear."

I finally had their attention.

"First, the immediate problem," I said. "The little man in the buckskins is named Rufus Messenger. He's a wrangler with a pickup cattle drive, He told me he'd had words earlier with the goon he killed. Messenger finally told me the goon is named Walter Demko, and he's head of a gang of sorts. The name rang a bell, so I went through the pile of circulars I'd stuffed into the desk drawer and they are serious goons, involved not only in rustling but strong-arm thefts and intimidation."

Carmody had refocused the astronomer's gaze he adopts when he's evading eye contact with me and tapped the table with that absurd finger.

"And who's the guy *you* killed?

"His brother," I said. "Messenger doesn't know the first name, and doesn't know the name of the guy who threatened revenge, either. But Messenger swears the threat is real, and he's terrified of them coming back. And he says they will. For him and for me."

Carmody seemed offended.

"What about *me?*" he asked. "Don't they want to kill me, too?"

"I'm sure they do," I said.

"Wait a minute," Elmira said, emerging from her stone-face trance. "If this Demko is so tough, how'd that little butterball outdraw him?"

"Nipples," Carmody said.

Elmira turned to me, some animation and irritation returning to her face, which was moving almost like the face of a normal, non-stone human.

"Nipples," I said.

"Actually, the caps on the nipples," I continued.

"Actually," Carmody added, "when you come right down to the fact of the matter, it ain't so much the problem of the nipples *or* the caps, it's that danged hammer."

Elmira was beginning to steam, and I was enjoying it. It was interesting to see how she reacted when someone else was utterly incomprehensible. She had a habit of assuming that I could read her mind and fill in those vast blank areas that she expected me to magically absorb. It was nice to reverse the process.

"Belden had a Colt Walker," I said, knowing it would mean nothing to her.

I am not normally a vengeful person but I reasoned this would be a learning experience for her.

"It's a cap-and-ball model," I said, after a suitable pause. "Most people are turning over to metal cartridges but a lot of old-timers like to stick with what works, and by and large cap-and-ball models are dependable. But the Walker has a big, curved hammer with a lot of space between it and the frame."

Elmira growled.

"What about the goddamned nipples." It didn't come out like a question, exactly. More like an implied threat of grim consequences if I didn't explain.

"Yes," I said, "the goddamned nipples connect the powder with a percussion cap. The caps fit over the goddamned nipples in the cylinder. In the Walker the caps tend to fall off and drop way down into the mechanism. Because of the way that particular gun is built, sometimes you can't see them down in there but they can

keep the hammer from making contact and set-
ting off the round."

We were silent for a moment.

"Anyway," I said, "I don't know when
those Demkos will be back or how many of
them will come. Could be tonight, but I doubt
it. Storming a jail, if that's indeed what they are
planning, takes some organization and rallying
of manpower."

"You think they'd really do that?" Elmira
asked, although I sensed she knew the answer
as well as I. The awe-inspiring legal bulwark of
a one-cell jail and two lawmen in an isolated
town in the outskirts of the Backside of Beyond
did not cause most criminal enterprises to be
paralyzed with fear.

"Yes," I said, and took a breath.

Carmody made a spinning speed-up motion with that overgrown finger.

"You said there's something else. Could
you please drop the other shoe before they get
here and kill us?"

I took another breath, and neither of
them spoke until I finished.

It had unfolded at Courter Crossing, the
site of a Confederate fort and a military prison.
We'd heard sporadic reports of ghastly conditions at the prison, of shortages, starvation, and
disease. Provisions were being siphoned off by
a corrupt quartermaster, John Brokenshire,

and his equally corrupt commandant, Joseph Lefler.

I was, for two months or so, Josiah Hatch, a purveyor of cloth and boots, ostensibly just as corrupt as Brokenshire and Lefler.

The army had found some real haberdashers and cloth merchants to give me a crash course in the fabric and foot-ware trade, but most of it was a waste of time. No one gave a damn about the fine points of my merchandise. It was the protocol of the kickbacks and the bribes that took some plausible negotiation, and that wasn't too hard to fake. Avarice is a universal concept, regardless of the commodity.

Intermediaries and impostors had established my cover and bona fides, and I spent a month insinuating myself into the game. At first, it was easy: I'd been bankrolled by Washington and a ready flow of bribe money buys you instant credibility.

I hadn't met Brokenshire, the deal-maker yet.

I'd heard he was canny, and I suspected that he thought something was up. I'd heard he was checking me out. Word got back to me from our spies who were pretending to be their spies, or maybe it was their spies pretending to be ours, or a double agent pretending to both. I lost track.

Spying can be very complicated sometimes.

And that's when a beautiful young woman named Solana Pixley took a liking to me. She lived in a comfortable house on the edge of town. When I'd first arrived in Courter Crossing I'd seen her in the local restaurant where I usually ate and passed her a few times on the street, and she took no notice. But one night when I was eating dinner alone she'd asked to join me at my table.

All of a sudden, she was positively *mesmerized* by me. The details of my background were of infinite interest to her, and as the liquor flowed her questions grew more detailed, and it soon became obvious that the ultimate goal of the evening was to get me drunk and lure me to her bed.

The second part of the plan worked out, but I'd poured out a lot of the liquor when she wasn't watching. A lot of it went in my boot, which I emptied a couple times when I left the table to relieve myself.

Later, when she feigned a deep, alcohol-induced sleep, I did the same.

The light of a full moon was slanting through her bedroom window when I opened one eye just enough to see her get up, dress herself, and take my gun from the belt I'd slung across a chair.

I thought for a second that she was going to try to shoot me. I could live with that, literally: I'd unloaded the Smith and Wesson earlier in the evening. The Cooper Pocket double-action I'd stealthily transferred from my coat to the pillowcase before I pretended to fall asleep had all five chambers loaded, however.

She didn't attempt to shoot. She tucked the gun under her armpit, carried her shoes in one hand, and padded out the door. I fought the urge to look out the window. It was bright enough that I might be seen.

So I got dressed and circled around back of the house. I'd travel a wide arc and try to flank Salona, who I suspected was meeting with conspirators. I further suspected that those conspirators had, while I was otherwise occupied, used the time to sort through the belongings in my hotel room.

They'd want to compare notes and figure out if I were for real, and if I were not, kill me.

Maybe they'd even kill me just to be on the safe side.

But there was nothing in my room that would give me away. My rifle, extra ammunition and black night-time mission clothes were safely hidden in a hollow log a few hundred feet into some woods near the river.

If Solana planned to meet with Brokenshire, she'd save me a lot of trouble. I might get lucky.

I get lucky a lot. My commander, Major Thaddeus Munro, had told the general who'd recruited me for this operation that I was the luckiest soldier he'd ever met. Things just worked out for me, Munro said, according to the general's account of the conversation. Maybe, Munro had admitted during the conversation, I actually made my own luck, but either way I most improbably survived when that outcome seemed unlikely.

I never learned the name of that general nor did I ever see him in uniform. He was a spare, middle-aged man with grey hair and dark eyebrows who wore a banker's suit and met me in a tavern. He told me nothing about himself other than the fact that he didn't exist and the organization didn't exist.

And *I* would cease to exist if I accepted the mission and were captured.

The general – if he really was a general, a difficult philosophical dilemma because he actually, well, did not exist in the first place, according to him – told me that Munro had recognized that I was one of the "special breed" needed for this type of operation. *Special breed,* he said. It didn't come out like a compliment. It was more of a clinical description, the way you'd speak of a particular type of dog who was by breeding homicidally inclined toward a particular type of prey.

For two weeks I'd trained in secret at a remote barracks that I had been told, unsurprisingly, did not exist. I'd learned a new accent, details about the textile trade, some silly-sounding passwords and recognition signals, and I practiced shooting from extreme distance with the scope-equipped rifle.

Anyway, Munro was right about the lucky part. On the night Salona had set me up, the stars and the moon even lined up on my behalf, because it was so bright that I could hide behind a tree and see Salona and the man I took to be Brokenshire almost like it was day.

The size, age, and reddish-brown hair matched the description I'd been given of Brokenshire. He wasn't wearing a uniform.

I'd been warned that Brokenshire was clever and dangerous, but that remained to be seen. He was standing in a lighted clearing and hadn't noticed that an armed man had approached within twenty feet of him.

I wanted to do it quietly, and thought about trying to rush him by surprise and take him barehanded or with a knife. But he was standing on carpet of crisp fallen leaves and even the most oblivious bonehead could not fail to hear my advance. Also, what common decency that had not been bred out of special breed dictated that I make dead certain that it really was Brokenshire before I killed him.

I could have tried all sorts of fancy schemes – calling him by his first name as though I were a friend, hoping for him to betray himself through some recognition that confirmed his identity, or holding him at gunpoint while I searched for identification that he might or might not have.

I tried an easier approach. I'd been briefed on the roster for Courter Crossing and he was the only officer who held his particular rank.

Lowering my voice as far as I could without hurting myself and barking with that air of presumed God-like authority so beloved by senior officers, I bellowed: *"Lieutenant!"*

He actually started to say *yes, sir* before he caught on and immediately went for his gun.

I drew mine, but not in time.

I'd make a mistake and underestimated him. He was cat-quick and had ducked behind Salona. He held his sidearm to her head.

"Drop your gun," he said, ducking his head behind her head and shoulder, leaving just one eye exposed, "or I kill her."

He just assumed I would obediently drop my weapon out of chivalry for a woman who had betrayed me so, and then he could, of course, immediately cut me down. I knew he wasn't going to kill her; even if he wanted to, that would make no sense because he'd be casting aside his own shield.

So I shot between Salona's legs. I couldn't see their precise position of her limbs under the billowy dress but she was standing with her feet apart, attempting to keep her balance after

Brokenshire pulled her back toward him, and I took my best guess. She yelped; I'd grazed her.

But Brokenshire screamed. I'd scored a solid hit and shattered his knee. He fell to the left of Salona, scrambled to his good knee, and started to raise his weapon.

I put two rounds in his chest before he'd elevated his gun more than an inch or two.

Salona was hopping mad. Literally. Graze wounds hurt like hell and her face contorted to a mask of rage and she did a quick limp-and-hop step toward Brokenshire.

She was after his gun.

She had no real chance, and presumably knew it, but the pain of the wound had consumed her with the type of blind rage I'd seen on the battlefield. She was going to kill me or die trying.

I have to admit I admired her resolve. Not enough to let her shoot me, however.

But maybe it didn't have to come to that.

There were two guns in play: my Smith and Wesson, which she'd given to Brokenshire and he'd stuffed into his belt. She could reach it because he'd rolled onto his back before he died.

And there was Brokenshire's gun, a .45, on the ground in front of her.

Salona was making a life or death decision but she didn't know it.

My gun, or course, was unloaded, so if she seized it from the dead man's belt I'd have plenty of time to stroll over and grab it while she clicked away in futility. That would almost be fun.

But she dove for Brokenshire's .45, which had skittered a few feet in front of her.

She dove like she was starting a race on a lake.

For all intents and purposes, she was dead, a dead girl diving. After all, she clearly had the guts of a killer and wouldn't hesitate to use that weapon on me.

Only a sentimental idiot would let her live just because she was a woman with whom I'd recently shared a bed.

And, of course, that's what I did.

I fired at Brokenshire's gun, not with the intent of hitting it, even though I did. I just wanted to shoot in the dirt and scare her away from reaching for it.

I got lucky once again.

You can make trick shots like hitting a gun on the ground in broad daylight when you have plenty of time to aim and nobody is poised to shoot back, but it's a whole other story at night when your life is at stake.

The .31 balls in my Cooper don't have a lot of stopping power but they are lively little rounds and do a lot of traveling when they ricochet.

Before I ran back into the woods I tore off the sleeve of Salona Pixley's dress and saw that the round had entered her arm above the elbow and exited up near the top of her shoulder. Bullets do that a lot – hit a long bone, change direction, and slide along the surface of the bone until they exit.

I was going to use the scrap of dress as a tourniquet but there was no point. The entry and exit wounds weren't bleeding much and most of the blood that was leaking came from the shoulder, where a tourniquet wouldn't have been effective, anyway.

Salona was feeling about in that tentative way you do when you're not sure if all your parts are still there and you're not quite sure you really want to find out.

I knew that the wound wasn't serious and that in fact she'd been pretty lucky. Shoulder wounds often scramble the socket and impair you for good, but she'd been hit with a clean in-and-out that might not have broken any bone at all.

She didn't know that, and it would take her couple minutes to come out of her state of shock and figure it out, and that was plenty of time for me to gather up the small arsenal scattered about and disappear into the moonlight.

When I'd finished with my story, Carmody maintained his poker face.

"And you went gunning for Joseph Lefler, the commandant, right after you killed Brokenshire?"

"Yes," I said, "at first light. I was going to try to talk my way into seeing him with the offer of some sort of deal but obviously Salona would have given him the word about me by then. And maybe that wasn't even a factor. Union troops had been advancing inch-by-inch for several days and were on the verge of overrunning them."

Carmody nodded.

"So by the time I got there at dawn, they'd already cut and run," I said.

"But you had a shot at him."

"I did. I was on a small hill and found an easy tree to climb. Lefler was smart. Most everybody else left on horseback, along the trails. They all got cut down. Lefler scuttled into the woods and melted away after I missed my shot."

Carmody drummed his fingers on the table.

"And you obviously didn't cripple her none with the leg shot, though you don't know nothing about the shoulder. Maybe that's why she chooses that ramrod-up-the-butt type of style."

"Maybe," I agreed, for lack of anything better to say.

Elmira cleared her throat.

"Just so I understand the whole story," she said, "you didn't have sex with her again *after* you shot her, like you told me the first time."

"I never told you –"

And then I gave up the struggle.

"No," I said. "I did not."

That seemed to satisfy her.

Carmody then spoke carefully, choosing each word as though he were stepping on slippery rocks while walking across a stream.

"And you never told us about your little side career during the war because you thought we would think less of you?"

I normally don't like to talk in circles but I wanted to answer this in my own way.

"Do you remember the conversation we had after I killed that sentry?"

He nodded.

Carmody knew where I was going with this. When we'd first teamed up we'd gone on a mission to rescue Elmira's daughter. I'd had to get past a gang member standing watch in the dark.

I'd received training in sentry removal, as we'd called it, in my special-operations unit. I'd gotten pretty good at it, and had, in fact, invented a new twist to the maneuver and trained other soldiers in its use.

It involves digging the top of your head into back of the sentry's neck while slipping an arm across his throat and using the leverage to magnify the power of the choke. Done correctly, it is invariably fatal.

When I returned from dealing with the sentry, Carmody, waiting for me in the dark, had remarked that we'd better skedaddle before the sentry woke up. He didn't understand the fact that *I* didn't understand what he was talking about.

Carmody had assumed that I'd somehow managed to temporarily induce some sort of harmless slumber on an armed man who was there with the express purpose of killing us.

We'd never spoken of it directly since, and it was one of those unresolved issues that you just put on the shelf and assumed it will never be settled. While Carmody is certainly no shrinking violet when it comes to killing, he's got this hot-blood/cold-blood honor code that I suppose I recognize but don't fully endorse.

Now, sitting across the table, the issue paid us another visit.

"I understand," Carmody said.

It came out, *ahh unnerstayand,* slow and deliberate.

It didn't mean he approved, I guess.

Well, I understood him, too, and that was the end of it.

So we all took a breath.

Elmira, whose face to this point had been hard and immobile as the image on a coin, actually smiled. I guess she was happy now that she'd finally straightened out the sequence of events regarding Salona Pixley.

"What now?" Carmody said. "Are you going to kill this guy you think is Lefler?'

I was startled, not so much that he put it so directly but that I hadn't given much thought to it, having been distracted by the gunfight in the Spoon, the threat of deadly retaliation, and Elmira's slant-eyed glares.

"I don't think so," I said. "That was an order given in war, and I'm not a soldier anymore, and the president ended war-crime prosecutions, so I don't think there's much I can do, legal or otherwise."

"Fine points never stopped you before," Carmody said.

I let it pass.

"And I'm not completely sure it's him. But it makes sense. I know that's Salona. I'd certainly recognize her."

Elmira cleared her throat.

"And that adds to the likelihood that it's Lefler. He and Salona used to live in the same town, so it makes sense that they could still be associated."

"And they both wound up in a theater troupe?" Carmody said.

"Well, Salona did, for sure. I don't know what Lefler's business was before the war. Maybe they were both performers before. Maybe they took it up after. But one thing's for sure: Lefler's not going to admit to his real identity, if that indeed is who he is. And I doubt that Salona will give anything up, either."

"Unless you threaten to shoot her again," Elmira said, in a helpful mood.

"You never know how people react until you confront them," Carmody said. "If I was you, I'd spring it on her right now. They're all staying at the hotel. I imagine she'd be in her room by now."

Elmira's expression again became as rigid as Lady Liberty on the five-dollar gold piece.

"That would give you a nice chance to *re-connect*," she said. She was biting off the ends of her words again.

"Let's go see her together," I told Elmira.

"You want a chaperone?" she said.

"No, I want a witness," I said, and it was mostly true. The very last thing on my mind was rekindling a romance that never really involved romance with a woman who'd tried to kill me.

"She can say anything in front of me and then deny it later," I said. "Besides, you being there will be unexpected. It might throw her off."

Elmira didn't look convinced but her face was regaining some flexibility.

"Why not Tom? Wouldn't a deputy be a better witness?"

"First of all," I said, "somebody has to stay at the office and guard the jail and the prisoner. We've just killed two members of a criminal enterprise and a surviving member indicated he'd be back with reinforcements, looking for revenge. That might never happen, Or it might happen tonight."

"Makes sense," Carmody said. "What's the second reason?"

"I can't tell you," I said.

They both looked at me, their expressions more surprised than curious.

"I can't tell you because I don't know," I said, turning to Carmody. "It's just a hunch that it would be better if I kept you under wraps for the time being."

Carmody gave me a funny look but nodded. I wondered if what I'd just told him – and what I *hadn't* told him in the two years we'd worked together – would change how we'd function in the future.

I wondered if Elmira, who certainly had a past of her own, would trust me again after learning that I'd once used sex as a weapon, a ruse to counter a ruse, and culminated the relationship with gunshots.

Just to complicate things, a decade ago, which was a lifetime ago, I'd promised the government that I'd keep the story a secret and I had, until now. I wondered if that obligation still held. If so, what about my direct orders to assassinate Joseph Lefler?

So I wasn't quite sure where things stood when I looked at Carmody, then at Elmira, and then back at Carmody.

"We're wasting time," Carmody said, getting to his feet. "Before you go to the hotel, I suggest you pick up a rifle or two from the office and take it with you. Not that you need more stopping power for Salona this time around. But if there's trouble we may need firepower in a hurry."

Elmira bustled around the table and patted down her skirt.

"Let's go get a confession out of that cloghopper," she said.

I stopped by the office, with Elmira in tow, on the way to the hotel. Messenger was in the corner cell, looking at the floor, forlorn at the injustice of me locking him up but terrified at the prospect of getting out. He might have a point either way. I'd already explained to him that for now jail was the safest place he could be, and that Carmody would be along soon to stand watch.

Messenger had sighed and whined "all right," elongating it to a good ten seconds, and then resumed moping.

After some negotiation with the fussy lock I unfastened the chain that secured the agile little Winchester lever-action I'd come to favor lately, and handed it to Elmira. She seemed happy that I'd given it to her, but I explained that I didn't want her to shoot anybody with it – including Salona.

As Carmody had said, I needed some firepower with me, and needed an extra hand carrying it.

For no reason I could put my finger on I retrieved a Sharps rifle, pretty much the same model I'd used in the attempt on Lefler. It did not, of course, have a silly telescope screwed to it. My Sharps was damn near four feet long, weighed ten pounds, and had been chambered to accept a huge buffalo-size cartridge.

"Can I carry the big one instead?" Elmira asked.

She was starting to worry me, but I couldn't figure out a reason to tell her no. And if she wanted to lug around that cannon, she was welcome to it.

I shooed her out quickly. I didn't want her to remember that the bodies of the two people who'd died in her tavern earlier in the evening were now rolled up in blankets and stashed in a corner.

When we got to the hotel, I woke up the manager, who gave me keys to Salona's and Lefler's room. There was no one on the register named Lefler, of course, but the clerk knew who I meant when I asked for a short, heavy man with cold eyes.

The manager assured me I meant Joseph Layton.

Yes, I said that would be right.

Joseph Layton.

Of course. Who would have guessed?

The manager told me they were both on the penthouse level, which I thought was a rather pretentious way of referring to the second floor of the two-story hotel.

He looked a little worried when he noticed Elmira hefting the big buffalo gun but I assured him that there was no trouble.

Then Elmira said, "Let's go get her," and the manager looked a little panicky and quickly recused himself to the back room.

I didn't knock. I wanted the element of surprise on my side. The less time she had to plan her reactions and lies, the better.

I put the key in the lock and tried to turn it a softly as I could, but the tumblers wouldn't turn because the lock was already opened. I'd stayed in this hotel for months, before gradually migrating to Elmira's room above the bar.

I'm not particularly handy with things mechanical and fought with every lock on every door on every room I'd occupied, so I knew exactly how they were supposed to work.

This was odd, I thought, a single woman leaving a door unlocked in a place like this. Nobody does that.

Normally I stand to the side of a door when opening it and then sidle in when I see everything's clear, but that would spoil my dramatic entrance.

So I marched right in and almost stumbled into Salona Pixley.

Elmira was so close behind me that she bumped into me.

Elmira gasped.

It took me a moment to make sense of the scene. In a flash of mindless incomprehension I wondered why on earth Solana was dancing, and how she held herself so high in the air like that, with her body still stiff and her hands by her side.

And then I realized that she was hanging from a beam on the ceiling, a sash around her throat and an upturned chair on the floor about two feet away from her feet, which still were thrust into those silly wood-sole clogs.

"My God," Elmira said, reaching for her. "Get her down."

I blocked Elmira with my outstretched left arm, which still held the Winchester, and drew my revolver with my right.

There was no chance anyone was still in the room, but instincts and training have kept me most improbably alive for quite a while, and I see no reason to ignore them.

The room was only about eight by ten feet. There was no closet, only a rude wardrobe too small for anyone to hide in. The bed was ten inches off the ground, tight quarters under which to hide, but not impossible for a thin person. I knew from painful experience that the bed was of wood-slat construction, lighter than a bed with a frame, and was equipped with a laughably thin mattress.

A shove with my toe slid it into the wall.

There was nothing there except a chamber pot.

I moved Elmira to the side and surveyed the hallway again. It was dim, lighted by the same type of wall-mounted oil lamp that still flickered in Salona's room, but there was no movement, no open doors, and nowhere in my immediate view for anyone to hide. We'd come up the only staircase and hadn't encountered anyone.

"Please," Elmira said, "help her."

It hadn't occurred to me that Elmira thought the girl could still be helped.

"She's been dead for at least two hours," I said.

"How do you *know?*" she asked, exasperated, and began to cry.

I wasn't anxious to answer the question because my intimacy with death would reopen wounds that hadn't even begun to heal yet, but under the circumstances I didn't see any other options.

"The color and the rigidity," I said. "And the purple stain on the back of her neck. That type of stain takes at least an hour to develop."

I made a show of feeling the wrist for a pulse, even though the limb had already stiffened up so much that I'd have better luck finding a pulse in a tree branch.

"Can't you *please* take her down?" Elmira asked. "Don't you want to help her?"

"There's only one way for me to help her now," I said, "and to do that I have to look at the scene."

"The *scene?* I know you didn't mean for it to happen. But this girl killed herself because of *you*. And now you want to stare at her?"

I ignored her and walked a slow circle around the dangling body. The light was dim on the side away from the light and I had to rotate her as she hung from the beam. Then I lifted her skirt.

"My God," Elmira said. "What are you *doing?*"

"Helping her the only way I can. Finding her killer."

Elmira is not particularly squeamish. Admittedly, she'd spent two whole days throwing up after seeing the aftermath of a gunfight in her bar a few days after I'd first arrived in town to investigate the death of the former marshal, Billy Gannon.

Gannon had been captain of my unit in the war, and he'd left word for me to be summoned if anything happened to him, which it did, thanks to a gunman who most conveniently knew to ambush Gannon from his blind side. I knew that the gunman knew that Captain Gannon had lost sight in one eye during the war, and while it would have been a tough case to prove in court, the gunman saved me the trouble by drawing on me and kindly allowing me to kill him and put him and the investigation to rest.

The incident in her bar involved a gang that was indirectly involved in Gannon's death. The incident also involved Carmody's shotgun. It produced a mess that even made me gulp a couple times to get my digestive tract moving in the right direction after the smoke cleared.

Elmira calmed down after I'd cut the sash the held Elmira dangling in the air. The sash belonged to a robe I'd found in the room's wardrobe. I set the body on the bed, arranging it in a rough approximation of a sleeping position.

She didn't' want to look but eventually relented when I insistently showed her the two sets of marks on Salona's neck. One mark was whitish, and was deep on one side of the neck and angled up high on the other, just as you'd expect from an indentation made by hanging a body. The other mark, though, was darker, the color of a bruise, and was level. It stretched all the way around the neck.

In other words, one mark was from hanging. The other was from being strangled.

Elmira became lost in thought, and actually touched Salona's neck, feeling the deep furrow left by the horizontal ligature.

"How do you know the strangle mark didn't happen after? I mean, I know it doesn't make sense to strangle a dead body but nothing makes sense about this."

"I know for two reasons," I said. "The mark that you'd get from hanging a dead body would be white. Bodies don't bruise much, if at all, after the blood stops flowing. But the strangle mark is a deep bruise from bleeding under the skin, so that's the one that happened – started to happen, anyway – when she was alive. Second, the strangle mark is a lot deeper than the hanging mark. Either strangling or hanging will kill, but when people strangle a victim they often do it with a lot more force than is really necessary. The throat and neck is soft tissue and it doesn't take much to collapse it and cut off the air, but someone who's inexperienced doesn't know that."

Elmira nodded.

I held up a finger and then, with a start, realized I was acting just like Carmody and drew my hand down. I actually hid it guiltily behind my back, such is my distaste for the gesture.

"There's more," I said. "She lay on her back for a while before whoever did it strung her up," I said, pointing to the back of Salona's neck. "Right after a person dies the blood gathers at the lowest point of the body. If she'd been hanged to death, the pooling blood would have turned her feet and ankles purple, in the front and the back. But the only purple color I've seen is here on the back of her neck and on the back of her legs."

"Salona!"

The voice in back of me startled me and made me angry at the same time. I was mad at myself for losing track of my surroundings after getting carried away with my lecture, like a certain elongated deputy of my acquaintance.

It was a booming voice that filled the room and when I whirled I pointed my revolver about a foot higher than it belonged.

The voice belonged to the little man who had played the violin during Salona's clog dance and performed the Shakespeare reading.

He'd been standing up on stage during the performance and the perspective threw me off. He was even smaller than I'd perceived. He was only about an inch or two over five feet tall. He had a huge head, however, balding on top but haloed with wiry gray hair that stuck out in coils about six inches on each side.

The little man didn't jump or raise his hands. Instead, he swept the room with his eyes and then looked squarely at me.

"You're the marshal." It was a gentle voice.

"Yes. I know you were in the show, but I don't know your name."

"My name is Ben Jaffe. Mrs. Adler knows me; I was the one she spoke with when she hired us."

The little man picked up the sash from the floor and looked up at the other half knotted around the small beam supporting the eave of the top-floor room.

He shook his head.

"She's not the type to kill herself," Jaffe said.

"She didn't," I said. I probably should have played it cagey but decided, on instinct, to go the direct route.

"I think somebody strangled her and then staged the hanging," I said.

Jaffe gave me a level stare. Not shocked, not challenging, just attentive.

"Do you suspect anyone?" he asked.

"You, for starters," I said, and watched for his reaction.

"Yes, that would make sense, wouldn't it? Criminals are often drawn back to the scene to admire their handiwork. You often find the arsonist among the fire brigade. And if I wanted to establish my innocence the first thing I would do is show up and act surprised, wouldn't I?"

And that was all true. And I wondered how he knew it.

"Did you work in the law at one time?" I asked.

"I've always been an actor, and only an actor," he said, his voice filling the room even though he made no effort to raise it. "I trained in New York and London, and while I'm currently appearing in...well, *this place...*"

"Shadow Valley," I said.

"Yes, even though I'm now performing in this *place*, I have long experience, during which I've studied parts and literature and people and their motivations. The jobs of being an actor and being a marshal probably have more in common that you might think."

Sometimes Elmira can't help herself from making comments.

"He probably spends more time putting on an act than you do," she said.

I was going to glare at her but I was saving my menacing stare for Jaffe.

And he picked up his cue and put my theory to rest.

"The problem with that theory," he said, "is my stature. Not my stature as an actor, but my physical stature. I'm afraid the two are inextricably linked, but that's beside the point."

He spread his hands as though the situation was perfectly obvious, which, as it finally penetrated my skull, it was.

"I would not be able to string up a dead cat," he said. "Or a mouse, for that matter."

He had me there. That did not rule out him acting in concert with others, but that didn't seem likely.

So I asked him about the other members of the cast and crew, which only amounted to six people.

I got to asking about Lefler – *Layton* – last. I didn't want to seem anxious and tip Jaffe off.

The little man with the big voice shrugged and told me that Layton kept to himself and was the troupe manager, even though he, Jaffe, took care of the bookings with the theater owners.

Layton was a powerful man who could hire and fire at will, Jaffe said, and he added that he hoped I understood.

And of course I understood everything. Jaffe was scared to death of the stout man with the cold black eyes.

I told Jaffe that I wouldn't mention that I'd spoken with him.

I didn't know exactly how I'd get the truth out of Layton/Lefler, but he didn't look like the type who'd scare easily, and he probably knew enough of the law to know that I couldn't have much of a case – either for the death of Salona Pixley or those long-ago atrocities in Courter Crossing.

You didn't have to be a Pinkerton to fill in the blanks of a pretty plausible theory. Salona had told the man who now called himself Layton who I was and how she knew me. Layton reasoned that because I'd never met him, as far as he knew, I couldn't identify him as commandant of the camp but Solana *could*.

And that's why she was dead.

And I had two cases that I had absolutely no way to prove. Maybe someday doctors and lawyers will get together and write textbooks that you can point to in court, but for now my ideas about blood and bruises were just the musings of a small-town marshal, and no judge or jury would take them seriously. So Salona's death would stay a suicide.

As for Courter Crossing, there wasn't any way I could prove that Layton was the man I'd seen in a telescopic gunsight for a moment a decade ago. I don't think there was any charge on which I could arrest him.

I *could* let it be publicly known who he was, which would not be a boon to his theater business and would likely put him in the path of a revenge-seeker's bullet someday.

I'm sure that occurred to him, too, and the death of Salona was an insurance policy against that.

But for right now, my hands were tied. If Layton was Lefler, I'd have to come up with more proof. And if I could, there was no legal way to hang anything on him.

I'd have to figure out a way to let him hang himself.

And I was about to knock on his door and improvise when I heard the hoof-beats.

There were seven of them, riding motley horses of uncertain ancestry, and three of them incongruously carried lighted lanterns.

On this end of town at about one in the morning the Spoon generally manufactures all the noise, and a lot of it. But because we'd closed early, the street was deserted and the sound traveled conspicuously. I imagine the riders hadn't expected the silence, because they slowed their horses looked around with self-conscious apprehension.

I was on foot, hugging the row of buildings across the street from my office, trying to stay hidden as long as possible. I'd taken both rifles from Elmira and asked her to stay put in her room. I carried the light Winchester and slung the overgrown Sharps over my shoulder.

I could see and hear them clearly, though I wasn't close enough to recognize any of the faces as being men I'd seen in the bar. They were well within rifle shot, but I couldn't just open fire on a group of horsemen just because they were riding late at night carrying lanterns they didn't need. The clouds had cleared completely when the cold snap started and you could probably read a newspaper by the light of the stars and the full moon.

It occurred to me that I didn't have a plan.

And then I saw that they obviously *did* have a plan. They threw the burning lanterns at the window of my office.

And, I observed, it was, unfortunately for me, a damned efficient plan. They wanted Messenger, and they wanted me and Carmody. They knew exactly where two of us would probably be and one would be for certain.

And they turned the tables on us.

Fighting your way into a marshal's office isn't easy, but if you flush the occupants out *they* are on the defensive, not *you*. The riders certainly knew there was no back door; they would have checked that just by passing through the alley behind the building.

Most offices with a jail inside don't have backdoors, anyway. Ours didn't even have a back window in the cell any more. The former marshal, recognizing that windows, even heavily barred ones, invite the introduction of contraband, including guns, had bricked it up himself.

There were sturdy bars on the front window, in front of the glass, as well as over the small window on the front and only door. The riders could plainly see the bars from the street, but they'd probably thought that the thrown lanterns might hit between the bars, break some of the glass, and spew the fiery liquid inside the room.

It didn't work out that way, but it hardly mattered. The lanterns – big railroad-type devices, as far as I could tell – spewed their contents on the boardwalk in front of the window and door.

There was a surprisingly loud *wuffff* sound and tendrils of flaming liquid began to move like creeping fingers.

The boardwalk was sloped for drainage so some of the kerosene or coal oil – I'm not sure which fuel these lanterns took and I don't really know the difference anyway — spilled into the street. But a lot didn't, and in a few seconds those dry, half-rotted walls would catch like kindling.

Carmody and Messenger would be incinerated, unless they bolted out the front door, in which case they would be cut down by gunfire.

My first thought was how I could get to the fire barrel.

But how could I dip water out of it and douse the flames when I'd have to stand directly in front of seven armed men who were there for the express purpose of perforating me?

Apropos of nothing, a line from the Rime of the Ancient Mariner went through my head: *water, water, everywhere.*

But in my case, not a drop to throw.

We had more than a dozen fire barrels in town, and I religiously kept the one in front of my office full to the brim – not only because of the ever-present threat of fire but because previous generations of fire barrels had saved my life twice when I ducked behind them while being shot at. Water dissipates a lot of energy from a bullet, and in one encounter the barrel to the left of the door had absorbed five rounds of pistol fire until I had to seek new cover after it broke apart and...

"*Shit,*" I said out loud, not caring if they heard me.

They'd hear from me soon enough.

I shouldered the monster Sharps and put three rounds into the barrel, aiming for the lower two hoops.

The Sharps is a single-shot weapon but if you work it fast — and I could, because I've had a lot of practice – you can squeeze off a round a second.

Those giant buffalo-hunting rounds, tearing the bottom reinforcements apart, damn near made the barrel *explode*. I can't swear to it but I think I saw the staves fly asunder and leave, for a fraction of a second, a mass of water floating in the air before gravity took over and it hit the boardwalk with a mighty splash.

So now I had a clear understanding of the intent of the men. They weren't out for an innocent night ride. And I had a rifle in my hands, and every justification in the world to use it.

So I did.

The three who threw the lanterns made an amateur mistake: They had stopped to admire their work. Had they just thrown the lanterns and immediately turned away they would have ridden into cover.

I resisted the temptation to admire my demolition of the fire barrel, even though I was concerned about whether it would really quench the flames. I immediately turned the Sharps on the rider closest to the cover of the buildings. I could see only his shoulder and hat obtruding from behind the corner wall of the feed store.

You usually want to go after the hard targets first because you'll have a second chance at the ones in the open. If you give into temptation and shoot first at the targets in the open, the ones able to hide more quickly will do so, and you might never get them.

I aimed for the exposed shoulder but then thought better of it. I remembered that Carmody, in one of his recent spates of repairing various structures, including the recently rebuilt ranch house of his girlfriend, had lectured me on the shortcomings of construction in these parts. Most of the slapped-together buildings don't have posts on the corners. The walls, usually of thin planking and siding, are basically held together at the floor and the ceiling. So I adjusted my aim about a foot to the left, where his chest would be behind the corner of the building, and let loose.

I heard a scream and saw the brim of the hat jerk and then I heard a body thud to the hard-packed ground. The rider farthest toward the center of the street, the one who had thrown the first lantern, took his eyes off the fire and started to spur his horse toward cover, but it was too late. I shot him in the chest before he'd moved a foot.

Then there were five of them.

I knew more or less where they were, for the moment anyway. They'd ridden behind the row of buildings on the next block on the other side of the office from where I was.

I knew what they were talking about, too, even though I couldn't hear anything but the ringing in my ears from the buffalo gun.

They needed to decide whether to press the attack or cut and run.

Their arson plot had fizzled, literally. The fire was almost out, at least where it mattered – on the boardwalk and the front wall. But the water from the exploding fire barrel had washed the burning stuff into the street, where jarringly out-of-place pools of blue and yellow flames flickered and cast a rainbow reflection in the oily water beneath.

And the Demko gang, if that was what they called themselves, probably worried that reinforcements would soon be on the way, so they had to decide what to do soon.

The truth that there were only a couple local men I could count on. One is the druggist, a spare, grey fellow of indeterminate age who'd served in two wars and keeps a sign in his window saying that due to the rising cost of ammunition he will no longer provide burglars with a warning shot. There was also the town blacksmith, a strapping young fellow who was ideal for a fistfight, but whose aim was so bad he couldn't hit water while standing in a boat.

Collective defense simply is not a priority in a community made up primarily of drifters and drunks, so Carmody and I were, at least for now, on our own.

The second decision facing the Demkos was whether to remain on horseback or pursue the assault on foot. A mount provides you speed and a means of quick escape, but horses are not exactly stealthy animals. They plod, they stomp, they whinny, and they snort – usually when you most want them to keep quiet.

In the middle of the night on deserted streets you might as well have sleighbells on them.

I wasn't sure if one or more of the men still had the office door covered, but I would have bet that they did.

Carmody's options were limited. He had to maintain some distance from the window or he'd be an easy target. But he couldn't let the Demkos get up close. If they stormed from the front, or snuck up unobserved from the side, and suddenly started firing through the window, he had nowhere to hide.

But Carmody had heard the shots and probably seen the horsemen drop, so he knew I was out here, and that the Demkos would be unlikely to do much sneaking around in direct view of the office.

So right now Carmody would be keeping away from the window, biding his time, and probably wondering if it was time we put a back door in the place. I don't like the idea of creating another way for people to sneak up on me, or for criminals to get out, but this was the second time in a year that we'd had good reason to want to hightail it but had a brick wall in the way.

That brick wall, built by persons unknown in years before even the oldest current residents came to town, was just about the only piece of decent construction in a town slapped together more or less at random.

The building was fashioned of walls of vertical slats that were nailed together on the ground and then stood upright and fastened to a roof. Window and door openings had been cut in after the walls were erected, sawed out sort of freehand, as they bore only a passing resemblance to rectangles and squares.

To this model of modern architecture, horizontal siding – usually from any scrap that could be scavenged – had been nailed on the outside.

The brick back wall only ran in back of the marshal's office, not on the millenary shop that shared the side wall to the left, as you faced the building, or the cigar store that adjoined on the right. And as with most other things in Shadow Valley, even the decent portion of the construction fell victim to over-arching stupidity: The brickwork had been constructed on the *inside* of the slat wall, with the bricks sitting *on top* of the same rotting floor that lay directly on the termite-infested soil beneath.

But the bricks themselves were nicely pointed and sturdily connected to the left and the right wall of bars that formed the cage of the cell. My guess is that many years ago the town fathers had jailed a bricklayer or a mason and let him work off his sentence through skilled labor. Maybe they'd locked up an iron-worker, too: The bars themselves were thick and still rust-free and unlike most of the construction in the rest of the town they actually *did* form rectangles.

The long and the short of it was that even if the Demkos made it into the office they'd find it impossible to extract the prisoner from the cell for lynching purposes. But I doubted they would insist on a ceremony. They'd could content themselves with blasting him through the bars.

I'd waited several minutes, finally positioning myself in the doorway of the general store, a vantage where I had a good view of the office and both ends of the street in front.

Nothing was happening.

The fire was out.

The mounts were somewhere out there, making sniffs and snorts and other moist horse-sounds in the distance, but they weren't moving.

I was in no hurry. We could wait all night, and all the next day, for that matter, but they couldn't. Sooner or later help and witnesses would arrive. If the Demkos wanted Messenger, or me, or Carmody, or all of us, they'd have to act soon.

There were five of them left alive, and I'm sure none of them expected things to work out this way. When you rode into hick towns with hayseed marshals and threw burning oil on the jail, everybody was supposed to turn pale and give you your way.

If they were smart, they'd leave now. But now they were mad and thirsting for revenge and maybe drunk, which equals stupidity.

I waited a minute more.

And then hell opened up.

I couldn't figure out what was happening.

The shots were muffled, but they roared like a brace of light artillery, one after the other for a good ten seconds. I could feel the explosions resonating in my chest. If I had to guess, I would have pegged the sound as a shotgun with a heavy load, but something was *off*.

I couldn't tell where it was coming from. I couldn't pick up the usual cues of reverberation and echoes, and couldn't place the source.

And then I saw the glass in my office window shatter as I heard the muffled crack of what I thought was rifle fire. But I detected the angry buzz of bullets with perfect clarity.

I set down the Sharps and ratcheted the nimble Winchester, crouched down, and took a small step into the moonlit street.

That's when I figured it out: The shots – from the shotgun and the rifle – were coming from *inside* my office.

I heard another crack and saw a bullet burrow into the hard-packed dirt of the street, kicking up enough debris to make a clattering sound as the particles hit the storefronts across from the office.

It was a strange time to contemplate such a thing, but I marveled at the fact that in all my years of involvement with gunplay, I'd never before heard the sound of gunfire from *inside* a building while I stood outside.

There's good reason for that. *Nobody* shoots a shotgun inside a closed office and then blows out his own front window with a rifle when there's nobody outside to shoot at.

No one except Carmody.

Suddenly it was silent again.

I heard shouts in the far distance. People would be waking up now. They had to, now.

I'd fired the Sharps twice, two rounds close together, about five minutes ago. But people sleep through or ignore one or two isolated shots. When they wake up they're unsure of what they heard, think it's thunder or a dream, and go back to sleep.

But after the latest fusillade, the residents of the cemetery were probably sitting upright.

And then, suddenly, there was a creaking sound, so out-of-place and unexpected that it seemed somehow louder than the gun barrage, as the front door to the office swung open.

There was no one behind the door.

And *nothing* happened.

The door swung a little in the breeze, creaking again. The wind had picked up and it was getting colder.

The door almost blew shut, slapped against its frame, and then returned to its natural position when unlatched – open toward the street, leaning in the direction that most of the sorry old building tilted.

A minute passed, then another.

I thought I head footsteps – human, not horse – but couldn't be sure because now the breeze was rustling some leaves and hissing down the center of town, spitting the street-dust against wood.

The door creaked and slapped as every few seconds it blew almost shut and then opened again, as regular as the motion of some sideways eyelid.

Was the open door an invitation from Carmody? Did he want to lure the gang in? Why?

I realized that the door had me *hypnotized.* I forced myself to take my eyes off it and surveil the street, and in the moonlight I could just make out a massive shoulder peeking from around a corner two blocks past the jail. That would be Oak, the blacksmith, probably armed with his trusty and beloved .22, which could knock over a squirrel if the squirrel were of a dainty species and off-balance at the time of impact.

I was willing to bet that the druggist, Vern Miller, would be out there soon. Miller lived across the river, normally a five-minute ride, but ten for Miller, who plodded on a spindly, sour-faced horse that had somehow taken on the demeanor of its owner. But despite his stooped shoulders and pickle-sucking face, the mysterious Miller – who could have been anywhere in age between 65 and 110 – could shoot with deadly accuracy. He had a battlefield calm and command that had been honed in circumstances unknown and unspoken. Like many men who'd seen the fury of combat, he didn't talk about it much other than to change the subject.

Another gust caught the door and it slapped against the frame.

I started at the noise, and damn near slapped myself across the face to bring myself back to reality.

I took a deep breath and crouched and began to move forward.

If there's one thing I'd learned in combat, it's the importance of "watchful waiting." Those were the words used by our commander and drilled into us in training. You need patience, you need to stay relaxed, but above all you need to be attuned to your surroundings.

"Kindly don't shoot me," Carmody whispered in my ear, and I literally jumped off the ground like a startled cat.

"Jesus *Christ*," Carmody whispered urgently, waving his hands in a tamp-down gesture, "don't make no more noise and *please* don't pee your pants."

All I could do was listen to the blood pound in my ears and wait until I could breathe normally again.

"Would you please," Carmody whispered, "stop sucking like a fish and get back under cover and keep quiet?"

"How..." I said, too loudly.

After hearing myself sputtering, I leaned in to whisper.

"How the hell did you get out here?" I said.

"I keep a change of clothes in the office," Carmody said, as though that explained everything.

I spun my hand in a quick circle in the universal speed-up gesture that let Carmody know he was driving me close to the edge.

He pointed at his feet. The eaves blocked the moonlight but it was still bright enough for me to see the moccasins Carmody wore for tracking. He'd had been a scout during the war, and could read terrain like you or I read a newspaper. Equipped with the soft footwear that lets you sense when something you're stepping on is about to go crunch, the giant could move like a ghost.

"But how did you get out of the office?"

Carmody looked annoyed with the obvious nature of my question.

"You know I been trying to fix the place up, especially them parts the termites chewed," he said.

I gave him the speed-up signal again and heard the rush of blood return to my ears.

"Parts of them bug-bit walls you could damn near stick your hand through," he said.

I just waited.

"Did a little remodeling with that new double-ought ammunition I loaded," he said, and patted the barrel of his shotgun.

"You must have heard," he said.

It came out, *you musta heeeered.*

In self-defense, I tend to paraphrase when I talk to Carmody. Repeating things back to him forces him to confirm that I've heard correctly.

"You're telling me," I said, not quite believing it myself, "that you blew a hole in the back wall with your shotgun?"

He put a finger to his lips.

"Not the back wall," he whispered, and leaned in conspiratorially. "Even this trusty old gal here couldn't blast through brick."

He glanced at the weapon, apparently to reassure himself that he hadn't offended it.

"There's a real rotten part down in back of where we keep the safe. I moved the safe, shot a good size chunk out, and crawled into the cigar store."

"Alone?"

"The safe really ain't that heavy."

I wasn't going to give him the satisfaction, so I waited.

It occurred to me that there were violent men here to kill us. I should turn my attention to that, I knew, but I wasn't going to let Carmody win this one. I'd wait him out if it killed me.

"Oh," he said, as though he was genuinely surprised, "you mean did I *leave* by myself."

He thought about it for a moment.

"Well, you know them dead bodies, they wasn't going nowhere."

I agreed and nodded.

"Incidentally, we need to do something about them soon because they is starting to stink."

"All right," I said. "We'll take care of them if we don't get killed."

Carmody nodded and took his time with the next part.

"Now, as to Messenger, I kinda pulled him through the hole. He's rather ample in the hindquarters and it was a close fit. Then we went out the side door of the cigar shop. I was going to tie Messenger up somewhere but he's so scared I don't think he'll come out from hiding."

"Where's he hiding?"

Despite the circumstances, I was getting drawn into Carmody's narrative.

"The outhouse behind the hotel. I told him none of the gang would search there, as the smell kind of repels casual visitors, and this time of night there likely would be no regular customers."

Carmody, having concluded his monologue on his own terms, turned serious and we went back to the business of survival.

"Before I left, I opened the front door to give them something to look at if they was watching, which I suspect was the case. You give dumb bastards like that something strange to look at, they'll get hypnotized."

I let it pass.

"So I'm pretty sure no one noticed us leaving the cigar store, Carmody said. "I reached through the hole and pulled the safe back as best I could. It's not like nobody's going to see the hole, but it ain't exactly obvious. I wanted to make sure that in case they came in right after they didn't see we tunneled next door. And then I saw your boot-prints and tracked you here. On a dry breezy night you get a fresh coat of dust on the road every few minutes. If you're lively about it you can get good tracks before they blow away."

I was going to talk about what to do next but the conversation was cut short when we both heard it.

The soft hoof-shuffles of horses when there's action about to take place.

Horses are smarter than most people give them credit for.

They do not, for example, stand slack-jawed staring at a door creaking in the wind.

Also, horses know when something is about to happen. When men get ready to ride the animals start to turn in little circles and paw the ground a bit.

So it was starting.

I knew that Carmody liked to climb, perhaps some hereditary trait he shared with the squirrels that he still favored as part of his diet, so I told him to get to the roof of the stable, which had a peaked hayloft and was the highest structure in town.

While he did that, I'd work my way down a couple doors farther toward the office.

If they decided to cut and run, we'd let them. Maybe we'd pursue another day, but it would be during the day, and on our terms.

If they stormed the jail, we'd announce ourselves and ask them to surrender.

And if they didn't, we'd have them in a perfect crossfire.

They had other plans.

They thundered around the corner single-file, in my direction.

Three of them broke toward me, hugging the side of the buildings as closely as they could, firing down the row. It was no secret that my shots had come from this direction, and for all I knew they could have heard me flop around when Carmody tried to give me a stroke.

It was a gutsy move on their part, and given what they knew – which did not include Carmody's escape – not a bad maneuver.

They'd expose themselves, of course, but if they laid down a barrage I'd presumably freeze in fear and retreat. The riders they left behind would fire through the office window and mysteriously opened door, either killing the occupants or keeping them busy, until I was disposed of and they could all go back and turn the place into a shooting gallery.

Or, I might try to shoot back, in which case I'd give up my position.

They opened up with a hail of cover fire.

It's not easy to bide your time when bullets are buzzing about you, but most shooters tend to over-estimate their odds of hitting someone when they are firing in the general direction of a target. And most people being shot at tend to over-estimate when they reckon the odds of being hit.

Let me put it this way. When they started shooting they were two hundred feet away. Firing revolvers from galloping horses they probably would miss, most of the time, anyway, even if I were standing in the middle of the street with a limelight shining on me.

What they wanted was to panic me, force me to run or give away my position.

But while I scare easily when it comes to mountain men in moccasins sneaking up on me in the dark, this was my element and I knew the odds and the territory and I crouched behind the barrel until they were right on top of me.

I'd moved up on them since the last time I fired and they didn't expect that I'd be so close. The first rider was actually looking and firing forward when he passed right in front of me.

I shot him in the temple. He fell backward and his horse, spooked, literally ran out from beneath him. The rider did a complete backflip and landed flat on his stomach.

These men had clearly never ridden in battle. There was a rider directly behind the first, much too close. The second rider pulled back and reined the horse to the side to avoid the body in the street, whether out of squeamishness about trampling a comrade or the very real possibility that his horse would stumble over the body.

His motives didn't matter. I was able to get off two shots to his chest while he dithered.

And the horse tramped the body in front of it, anyway.

The third rider hunkered down and charged directly at me.

It was a bold move, I'll give him that, and his best remaining option. He had the considerable bulk of the horse's head and neck to hide behind, and considering our close quarters the animal was as formidable a weapon as his revolver.

Whether that horse would have barreled up the boardwalk and ground me up with his hooves is an interesting question, but one that will never be answered.

The horse reared up when the rider's head exploded.

Vern Miller lowered the sleek German rifle we'd lent him during a rescue mission on which he'd accompanied me on a few months ago. I'd sort of forgotten that I'd borrowed the German rig from my former unit commander, who'd also accompanied us. Major Munro had "borrowed" it, along with an impressive arsenal of other weapons and a complement of Cavalry Morgan horses, from someone else – God knows who.

Texas is a big place, and things tend to get lost in the system.

Miller had a ritual after he shot anybody.

"Asshole," he said, looking with sour contempt at the man with the missing brainpan.

Down the street the two remaining gunmen were firing through the open door of the office.

I let them shoot. They'd use up their ammunition and maybe kill some of the termites.

They would have had to have heard my gunshots but their attention was occupied with the office and I don't think they knew that their compatriots were dead. One of them dismounted and ran through the open door, firing at ghosts and shadows.

There were no lights burning in the office, but the door was open and the street was bathed in a moon-low as bright as the night I'd shot Salona Pixley.

The gunman emerged, looking up at the rider, and shrugged.

And then Carmody told both of them to drop their weapons.

Both men turned in the general direction of Carmody's voice and one fired off a wild shot in the general direction of the hayloft.

Carmody cut them all down with two shots.

The rest of the night was busy. We retrieved Messenger from the outhouse, where he'd been cowering in what must have been a particularly long and nauseating nightmare.

He took a deep and appreciate breath when we returned him to the jail, which was superbly ventilated now due to the lack of glass in the front window and about a dozen new bullet holes. It was cold, though, and I offered him the blankets that were wrapped around the decomposing bodies.

He declined and fastened another button on the tight-fitting buckskin jacket.

And then he began a tirade, in that creaky, stricken voice of his, about how we'd ruined his life. The Demkos, he whined, would *really* be out for revenge now. They'd figure out a way to burn him alive or string him up or fill him so full of lead that the pallbearers wouldn't be able to lift the body.

It was clear that he blamed us for assuring that nowhere would be safe for him, ever.

Carmody and I pointed out that we'd spent the previous couple of hours stacking up dead Demkos like cordwood and there surely couldn't be many of them left, but he was inconsolable.

Then Messenger followed his unerringly accurate loser's instincts and decided to make things worse. He was wanted on state charges, he whined, for a train robbery that liberated a sizable load of gold belonging to Texas, which did not take kindly to its removal. And some of the gold was from Mexico, being shipped to Texas as payment for a land purchase. Mexico, he said, might want him too.

Messenger claimed he'd merely been a lookout, unaware that there was a robbery in progress, merely stationed along a pass and told to fire off three shots if he saw lawmen coming.

Messenger said he figured that this was not exactly honest labor, but denied being a conspirator.

Maybe, he pleaded, I could get him some easy time in a state jail as far away from here as possible.

He liked the dry climate in El Paso, he said, and then sobbed and collapsed on the cot.

"You would have found out anyway," Messenger lamented, which was one of the dumber things he'd said tonight, a true accomplishment. I suppose I should have taken it a compliment – his touching belief that I was a one-man Ranger division and had in my files a list and picture of every suspected criminal in the state, and I would diligently scour it after each and every bar-room shooting.

Now, things were a mess. Before he'd opened his mouth, I'd probably have figured out a way to book him on an assault charge and get him a couple months in a local jail a couple towns over.

I couldn't let him entirely off the hook. He had killed, in front of witnesses, a man who was raising his hands.

But the damn fool was confessing to being part of a robbery of state gold on route from Mexico and I again had no choice in that matter, either.

I figured I'd better get him off my hands before he confessed to shooting Lincoln, so I asked Oak, the blacksmith, if he could miss the rest of a night's sleep and travel to Austin and talk to Tom Harbold, a state constable who'd served with me in the war and was a friend. Harbold, who was paid in part based on the number of arrests he made, probably wouldn't mind the trip.

It was about a half-hour before dawn. I could tell because those annoyingly ambitious birds who find it necessary to anticipate the sunrise were chirping.

I'd spent a long night producing dead bodies and then picking them off the street.

But there was one more body to take care of, and as far as I know she still lay in her bed just as I left her, with her hands folded across her chest in a macabre imitation of slumber.

I stopped by the bar to see Elmira again before I returned to the hotel to take care of my business.

She'd swooped down on me right after the gun battle, while smoke still clouded the street, hugging me like a life raft, and when she observed I had no visible holes in me she melted into one of those crying jags of hers, the type where she actually can't breathe and gets dizzy.

Then, as is her wont, she mechanically switched identities and became an efficient businesswoman and supervised the removal of bodies from the street and their proper placement in the official morgue, which was, of course, the corner of my office.

Messenger started to complain again and reminded me that in the nicer state prisons inmates did not have to share accommodations with piles of bodies. I assured him that we would bury them soon, along with anybody else who pissed me off in the interim.

He got the message and shut up.

Salona's body was undisturbed.

But the room was not. The door on the wooden wardrobe was closed. It was open the last time I'd been in the room, and I doubted if Elmira had closed it after I left – she doesn't even close her *own* drawers most of the time — so that meant that someone had been here tying up loose ends.

Looking for things he may have dropped in the struggle, maybe, or just reassuring himself that he'd not tell any tell-tales.

I'd screwed around with this case long enough, I told myself, getting distracted by homicidal gangs and stacks of dead bodies and whatnot. I wanted to confront the man who called himself Joseph Layton.

I remembered the room number and still had the keys I'd extracted from the manager in my pocket.

I was about to insert the key when I said to hell with being subtle. The hotel was as rickety as everything else in Shadow Valley and I just put my shoulder into the door.

The door wasn't damaged but a piece of molding split off the jamb in front of the lock and spun through the air, landing on the empty bed.

I was a little annoyed with myself for wasting time picking up the bodies and letting him get away. But I was the town marshal, and I couldn't very have respectable citizens — we had a couple, sort of — step over corpses in the morning.

There's actually a little more to it than that. To tell you the truth, I've got a problem with leaving bodies lying about.

The war had produced corpses in numbers that have never been rivaled in any history I'm aware of. If you look at it from that perspective, the numbers are staggering.

As a boy, my grandfather told me about *his* grandfather, who survived the Battle of Oriskany, one of the bloodiest conflicts of the Revolutionary War. I thus took an interest in Oriskany and read a lot about it in school.

While the numbers varied depending on the account, most of the books said that about four hundred Patriot troops died in that battle.

I was astonished by that number. I didn't believe I even knew four hundred people, and figured that was more people than lived in our whole county. I wondered how four hundred men could die at one time.

Not even ninety years later in Gettysburg, there were *three thousand* Union dead. It was close to that number in Spotsylvania, and more than fifteen hundred in Chickamauga.

I'd fought in smaller battles, but nonetheless we were overwhelmed with bodies, bodies strewn in layers so deep that we'd have to drag them aside to search for surviving wounded underneath, bodies that rotted and spread disease that killed more efficiently than bullets, and we were helpless to follow protocols that from my reading I knew that most armies adhered to through centuries – proper disposal of the dead.

So I'm allergic to leaving a body in the street.

And anyway, I don't think the man who called himself Layton would have gotten far. I doubt that a fellow of his proportions would rabbit away on foot, and stealing a horse is not as easy as you might suspect.

He had a horse at the stable, true. But getting a horse from the hostler in the middle of the night would have involved waking the cranky old man up and would surely have aroused suspicion. Especially when there was a gun battle blazing a few blocks away.

On top of that, picking your way through unfamiliar country at night, even a moonlit night, would not get you anywhere in a hurry, and blundering about in the dark makes it hard to cover your own trail. Pursuers who knew the trails, if they learned of your sudden departure and got suspicious, might set out to track you down.

I tried to put myself in the position of the man who calls himself Layton, the man I was almost certain murdered Salona Pixley and starved hundreds of Union prisoners to death.

First, he would certainly have known that I'd been in Salona's room.

No man kills a woman and then goes into a peaceful sleep down the hall and snores through a visit by a two hundred pound man in heavy boots clopping around on creaky floor-boards while carrying on a conversation with two people.

I imagine he heard most or all of the con-versation, at least Jaffe's end.

My guess was that he would wait until dawn, when he could retrieve one of the horses that had pulled the troupe's wagon. Nothing unusual about that at all. Many people set out at first light. He could claim business as usual – a meeting in Austin, maybe – and then disap-pear into the wind.

Truth be told, he could probably have stayed put and probably gotten away with it. I had no conclusive evidence that he killed Sa-lona, nothing that would persuade a judge, anyway.

Likewise, I couldn't prove that he was Commandant Joseph Lefler. And even if I could, President Johnson had declared the war over and put a halt to war-crimes prosecutions.

But the man *had* run. At least the bed was empty, and I can't think of any other reason why he'd be gone before dawn.

Maybe he'd run because he'd asked around about me, heard that I worked around the rules on occasion when the rules didn't square with what I thought was right.

We'd find out as soon as I got to the stable.

I turned the corner just as the first shaft of sunlight cut over the horizon and saw that he was leading a shaggy, unkempt horse out the front bay.

It occurred to me that I had not seen the hotel manager up and about when I returned to Salona's room, so I felt it reasonable to assume that the short man with the mean eyes had left without checking out.

So I arrested him for defrauding an innkeeper.

Messenger and Layton/Lefler both stood in the cell they shared, fists wrapped around the bars, glaring at me.

In a way, they could have been bookends. They were almost exactly the same shape and height. Both were balding and sported black beards with a dusting of gray.

But the similarities ended there. Messenger still wore the thick, rumpled buckskin, buttoned to the neck against the cool breeze that came in through the shattered window. The other man wore a vested suit with a glossy burgundy cravat. He appeared stylish but not very warm.

Messenger's glare was the hurt, indignant look of a spaniel swatted with a newspaper. The other man's eyes held the cold menace of a wolf's.

Layton/Lefler had spoken very little since I arrested him. He protested that he was intending to return to the hotel, and then he asked for a lawyer.

I told him that defrauding an innkeeper was one of the few laws that people in this town took seriously, that there was a lawyer who rode a circuit around these parts and he'd probably come in a couple days.

And then, in the same tone and pretty much in the same breath, I told him that I knew he'd killed Salona and that his real name was Joseph Lefler and that he'd been responsible for stealing provisions at Courter Crossing and starving hundreds of men to death.

He was damn good, I'll give him that. He exhibited a flash of puzzlement, the right dose of outrage and contempt, and a thoroughly convincing portrayal of the bewilderment of a man unjustly accused.

And then, after pretending to think about it for a perfectly reasonable amount of time, he came up with the perfectly reasonable observation that I couldn't prove any of it.

I told him that I sure as hell could.

And then I let him sweat, as much as a man could sweat in that cold cell wearing a fancy suit, until I figured out how I could actually do what I'd promised.

My first step was to roust Jaffe out of bed.

I told Jaffe what I needed him to do. And I said that unless he cooperated I'd arrest him for obstruction of justice. He blinked, probably realized I couldn't really do that, but took a close look at me and saw one pissed-off hombre who'd missed a night's sleep and was in no mood to screw around.

So he nodded eagerly, and said he'd go the wagon and get what we needed.

In my business, sometimes, it's a good thing to look crazy.

Carmody had found a pane of glass somewhere and was about to fix the window.

I told him to leave it alone for the time being. The cold snap is a good thing, I said, because it would give us some extra time before those bodies began to stink.

Besides, I told him, we had business to attend to.

Carmody is afraid of no man, including me, *especially* me, but he sensed that now was not the time to argue and followed me to Jaffe's room.

"This is goat hair," Jaffe said, as he set the blond wig on Carmody's head.

He probably expected Carmody to be startled or repulsed, but Carmody loves the taste of goat as well as most other creatures not customarily eaten by normal humans, and he smiled appreciatively into the hand-held mirror Jaffe had given him.

"On stage, it actually looks more natural than a wig made of human hair. But the actresses don't like goat because it smells."

Carmody sniffed the air.

"Seems all right to me," he said.

I swear he licked his lips, just a little.

"The beard is all right as dark as it is now, Marshal?"

"Yes, I said, "Gandolfsson was like a lot of Swedes. Blond hair but a dark beard. His beard was longer, though, and his skin was a lot lighter than Carmody's."

Gandolfsson was complected like a typical Swede, though his political leanings were unusual for the breed. Swedes and Norwegians had been brought over by the boatload to settle in railroad towns. Most of those towns were up North – some of them way up north in places like Minnesota – and the residents tended to be strong Unionists and damn fine soldiers. There was a crack Scandinavian Regiment that fought out of New York.

But Gandolfsson, I was told, came from a family of ironworkers who had somehow wound up in South Carolina, and the big Swede had become a Confederate officer.

"That's no problem," Jaffe said, dabbing some sort of smelly glue on Carmody's wiry beard. "We can just add some dark strands on. And maybe some gray? This was more than ten years ago, and the man, you say, was in his forties back then?"

I nodded. I like men who are good at their jobs.

"For the skin," Jaffe said, plucking a tube from a box, "we can use some of this stuff. It's called greasepaint. Getting very popular because it doesn't run or crack like powder. Powder gets creases when you sweat."

"I ain't the sweating type," Carmody said.

"But it also looks more natural in daylight," Jaffe said, spreading the goo with some sort of sponge, and then putting all his gear back in the box.

"You're fast," I said. "I thought this would take all morning."

"We have to be fast," Jaffe said. "In a show of the kind we do in, well, this type of *place*, an actor might play four roles in a night. You learn to do this in two or three minutes."

"There's one other thing," I said. "How do we make him look taller?"

Carmody was sitting down, but even in a seated position he was taller than Jaffe.

"Why on earth would you want to do that?

"Eric Gandolfsson was called 'The Seven Foot Swede.' He wasn't really seven feet tall, but he was taller than Carmody."

"How tall is Carmody?"

"I ain't no piece of damn furniture," Camody said. "You can ask *me*. I am six foot five and one-half inches tall."

I'd only met Gandolfsson once, when I was part of a raiding party that took him into custody. He was superintendent of another prison by then, having turned over Courter Crossing to Lefler about six months before. Gandolfsson swore that conditions at the camp were acceptable when he was in charge, claiming that it was Lefler who started siphoning off provisions.

I suppose it could have been true. Gandolfsson was tried after the war and acquitted.

Jaffe brought me back to the present.

"How tall was he?"

"Maybe six-eight."

Jaffe reached back into his box.

"We could stuff some of this springy foam into his boots, under his heels. Women use if it they need to make themselves look more...endowed," Jaffe said.

Carmody looked skeptical but shrugged and took off his boots.

"And if you want to make a character look taller," Jaffe said, "you put him in a tall hat. Does he have a tall hat?"

"Goddamnit," Carmody growled.

"Sorry," Jaffe said, very quickly, and made a point of looking Carmody in the eye. "Do you have a tall hat?"

"Several of them."

"Now the big question," I said. "Gandolfsson had a Swedish accent."

"Can he talk...sorry, Mr. Carmody, can *you* talk with a Swedish accent?

"Don't recall knowing that many Swedes," Carmody said.

"Foreign accents are not easy to learn," Jaffe said.

"Carmody is a natural showman and mimic," I said. "When he gets drunk and sings in the bar he can sing with no accent at all or sing just like an Irishman. And when he and Elmira don't know I'm listening he does imitations of me. Elmira gets hysterical."

Carmody cleared his throat and didn't object to the fact that I was talking about him.

Jaffe thought for a second.

"It's not that hard," Jaffe said, still being careful to look directly at Carmody. "Say the *J* sound like *Y*. So instead of saying *joke, say yoke.*"

"*Yoke,*" Carmody said.

"And instead of *yes* say *yah*," Jaffe continued. "Also, Swedes tend to say the *TH* sound like a *D*. They don't say an *A* sound like we say in *back*. They'd say *bock*. And remember that everything has an up and down lilt, and their sentences begin at the exact same pitch where they started."

Carmody nodded.

"So, '*yeah, that's a funny joke,*'" Jaffe said, "comes out, '*yah, dot's a funny yoke.*'"

"*Yah, dot's a funny yoke,*" Carmody parroted.

"He's very talented," Jaffe said, and Carmody growled.

"You're very talented," Jaffe said, quickly.

Jaffe looked at me, pleased.

"If you can tell me what you want him to say, we can go over it before his...performance. Maybe you should take a few minutes and write down his opening dialogue. You can't stumble at the beginning. And if you get them believing you right away, you can make a lot of mistakes later and the audience won't notice."

"I'll give you the first five lines now," I said. "Let's hurry."

"Really?" Jaffe answered, shaking his head a little. "Writing convincing dialogue, something that will fool a listener, is not easy. Do you think you can come up with a convincing lie off the top of your head?"

"Mister," Carmody said, pointing at me like I was the piece of furniture this time, "you have no idea who you're dealing with here."

I removed Messenger from the cell, telling him it was time for his outhouse break.

He told me he didn't have to go and he'd spent all night there, anyway, and didn't care to go back.

I told him to shut up, pulled him out of the cell, and locked the door behind him.

I held onto Messenger's collar and steered him toward the Spoon.

"Where are we going?" he whined. "Them Demkos might see me and come after me."

I told him I'd never met anybody who wanted to be in a jail so badly.

Then Messenger pouted some more and asked me if he could get something to eat. I told him that he'd been provided a more-than-generous breakfast ration just an hour ago, when Elmira dropped off a basket of bread and cheese.

"The actor guy stole it," Messenger said. "Said he'd kill me in my sleep if I didn't give it to him."

Somehow, that didn't surprise me.

It confirmed my suspicions, in fact.

And it filled in the last part of my plan.

I promised Messenger that he'd be perfectly safe in Elmira's back office, and that I'd scare up a meal somewhere.

Messenger brightened up, and asked me if the office had actual glass in the windows, because he was freezing.

I deposited Messenger at the Spoon and returned to the office. Messenger had given me another idea.

I nailed some canvas over the window.

"Cold snap," I told Lefler, "and it's getting worse. This ought to keep the wind out."

It kept a lot of light out, too, but I didn't light a lantern. You could still see enough.

Just enough for what I had in mind.

I could see both of them, but just barely, if I pressed my eye against the wall and braced myself to hold the awkward posture.

"They told me you'd be here," Carmody said when he walked into the room.

His lilting accent was subdued, not the broad parody I'd expected.

Lefler scrambled to his feet noisily, the metal of the cot scraping the floor. He reacted like someone had just thrown a pot of boiling water through the bars.

"Who *are* you?" Lefler said.

Maybe I'd just gotten into the habit of listening to speech tones during the few minutes that Carmody had received a master class on talking like a Swede, but it seemed odd the way Lefler said it.

In the same situation, I'd have said, "who are *YOU?*" – not, "who *ARE* you?"

"Who *ARE* you?" is the way you'd phrase it if you'd seen a ghost.

And I guess that Lefler had just done that.

"I can identify you, and I will," Carmody said.

Lefler looked around the office. He must have wondered if he was being watched, but there was nowhere to hide in my humble kingdom. There were two desks, mine and Carmody's, but you could see eighteen inches underneath them and unless a man had somehow wedged himself into a drawer and stayed there for several hours they didn't provide much of a hiding place.

And of course there was the office safe, which was now blocking part of my view and forcing me to hold a posture that I suspected would soon produce some sort of paralysis. I suppose a man could hide in there if he could fold himself into three sections and live without air.

It's possible someone could listen at the window, but it was fifteen feet away.

Lefler wasn't taking any chances.

He crooked a finger at Carmody and beckoned him to come closer.

Lefler's hand was shaking.

He waited until Carmody was six inches from the bars.

And then he spit in Carmody's face.

"Judas," Lefler hissed.

Carmody moved with slow deliberation as he extracted a handkerchief and wiped his face. He tucked it back in his pocket, dabbing it down with a dainty motion of the giant index finger.

And then his hand shot out and seized Lefler by the lapels. Carmody jerked him forward with such force that Lefler's doughy face was squeezed between two vertical bars.

"I've got nothing more to say to you," Lefler said. It was less than a whisper. More like mouth sounds without the propulsion of air, hard to hear over the ringing that still reverberated through the iron bars like the fading hum of an out-of-tune piano, after Carmody had slammed Lefler into the ironwork.

Carmody pulled harder and for a second I thought he might actually somehow mash Lefler's bones and pull him through.

Lefler moaned but said nothing.

Lefler shook his head, or tried to. It was pretty well wedged between the bars but there was a perceptible wag of the flesh of his cheeks.

And then Carmody kissed him on the forehead, released his grip, and stepped back.

We'd both heard enough, and the show was over.

Lefler hadn't admitted anything but his actions could be interpreted no other way. He'd been cagey to the end, not saying anything that could be used against him and making it perfectly clear that even if Carmody – Gandolfsson – crushed his skull no confession was forthcoming.

It didn't really matter. I had what I needed.

Carmody had only used one line of the dialogue I'd written for him, but he played it beautifully and deserved a curtain call. I'm not opposed to taking an occasional bow myself, and if nothing else I wanted to see how Lefler reacted when he saw me.

So I took my eye away from the edge of the hole in the wall between the office and the cigar store and braced myself to push the safe out of the way and emerge into the room, like the finale of a magic act.

But the safe, which Carmody had tugged into place when he escaped the office – and which he assured me wasn't that heavy – wouldn't budge.

I'm pretty strong. After the war, I fought on the bareknuckle circuit and won almost all my matches, and I'd wrestle as much as I'd punch. I was no match for the circus strongman types – those I'd circle away from and pop them with sharp jabs and crosses – but I held my own with most of the arm-twisters and neck-crankers.

I tried again and managed to move the safe about a sixteenth of an inch and then gave up.

There was nothing much else to do other than put my eye back to the narrow slit where the hole in the wall protruded beyond the edge of the safe.

Lefler had heard the sound and was looking in my general direction but I don't believe that he could see my eyeball.

"Termites," Carmody said, still employing his Swedish lilt, and walked out, closing the door gently behind him.

Oak returned with Tom Harbold early that evening. Harbold was leading a riderless horse to which he'd tie the prisoner.

Harbold and I had served in the same unit and held the same rank, though I was a few years older and had been commissioned before him. We weren't what you'd call close friends but we spoke the same language and were easy in each other's company. We'd get together every month or so, drink and talk, and sometimes drink and not talk.

As happens with men you've fought beside, you don't always need to put things into words to get your point across.

We shook hands and exchanged pleasantries and I paid Harbold two hundred dollars of my own money for transporting the prisoner. He showed surprise for a second, and then, as though reciting by rote, told me it wasn't necessary as he'd be paid the standard twenty-five dollar arrest and transport fee by the state, and there might even be a small payment coming from Mexico.

I told him it was worth every penny to have a man of his judgment and discretion handle the transport.

Then, almost as an afterthought, I told him all about what had happened. Harbold had heard of Lefler and said that it was too bad that tribunals had been ended, because any man that would starve prisoners and pocket the proceeds from the food he stole deserved whatever he had coming.

If the law was no help, Harbold said, then any alternative solution was welcome.

Our talk turned to the gold robbery and Harbold said he'd never heard of anyone confessing to such an old case. Nevertheless, he said, the wheels of justice must keep turning once they're started. He said he couldn't predict exactly what would happen to the guy.

Texas was a big place, and Mexico was even bigger, and there might be jurisdictional issues, and a fellow could get lost in that system forever.

Especially in Mexico.

Yes, I agreed, especially in Mexico. Mexico would be an ideal place to get lost.

I gave Harbold keys to the office and the cell door and asked him if he would mind getting Messenger himself because I still hadn't slept, which was true, had a headache, also true, and was freezing my ass off, which was exceptionally true.

Lock up when you leave and keep the keys, I told him. I had plenty of spares and I'd be up in Austin next week and get them back when I bought him dinner.

Harbold smiled. He loved good food, especially good *free* food. I can't blame him; who doesn't? Besides, for a number of reasons, I felt I owed it to him and was genuinely looking forward to it.

I also genuinely was looking forward to getting back inside. It had gotten progressively colder through the day and this was one of the coldest nights of any April I could remember, at least in Texas.

Harbold was wearing a snappy blue greatcoat with brass buttons and would have done fine in a January snowstorm in Maine.

He looked at his paperwork and told me he didn't mind handling the prisoner himself. He could handcuff a 50-year-old man who was five-foot-five, thank you very much.

I assured him that the other prisoner was about the same size, docile, and posed no threat.

Harbold gave me a look that told me he wasn't afraid of a hundred little men and to please stop wasting his time.

I advised him to gag the prisoner, too. Messenger was prone to yelling a lot, I said, and as all prisoners were pathological liars, nothing that would be said was worth listening to anyway.

"Noted," Harbold said, "for the record."

We nodded.

I resurrected the old joke about how it was so cold that his political bosses in Austin probably had their hands in their *own* pockets tonight, and I started toward the door.

"What about the prisoner?" Harbold said. "I don't want him to freeze to death during the ride. If somebody dies in my custody, I have to fill out a form."

"He'll be all right," I said. "He's wearing a heavy buckskin jacket. For the record."

Then something occurred to me, and I warned him to ignore the pile of dead bodies in the corner.

There aren't too many men who would take that in stride, but Harbold didn't even blink.

He nodded and rode off, with his riderless horse in tow, toward the office.

About a half-hour and two whiskeys later I walked from the Spoon to my office and looked in through the bars on the glass-free window. I'd taken the canvas down a few hours earlier when I'd returned Messenger to his cell, telling him and Lefler that I'd be right back to temporarily nail some wood over the opening and light the stove.

In all the excitement it had slipped my mind, I guess.

Rufus Messenger was in the cell hugging himself and stomping his feet.

"The son of a bitch stole my coat," he wailed.

"I figured he would," I said, and handed him a spare jacket that I'd retrieved earlier from someone who was no longer in need of it. Messenger either didn't see the bullet-hole and dried blood or just didn't care by that point.

Messenger's teeth were chattering but he had a story to tell.

"The guy in the uniform," Messenger said, "he thought the other guy was *me*. I started to tell him and he told me to shut up. Then the other guy tried to say something and the big guy in the uniform punched him in the throat and said he'd knock his teeth out if he said one more word. Then he gagged him and cuffed him and dragged him out. Like he didn't care who was who."

I shook my head and told Messenger that it's hard to get good help nowadays. Those state employees just want to fill out the paperwork and collect their fee.

"I didn't try to pull nothing, Marshal. But that big guy wasn't taking no guff. He looked like a stone killer."

I agreed. Messenger had done the right thing by keeping his mouth shut.

Keeping your mouth shut is often the best option, I said.

I told Messenger that this was all an embarrassment and I would appreciate it if he would just ride off and disappear, maybe to Arizona or somewhere a long way away.

And keep his mouth shut.

The Demkos were probably all gone, I assured him, but I couldn't be sure. I assured Messenger he'd be probably be safe around here but he'd be much better off with a change of scenery. And maybe a new name.

I'd get his horse out of hock at the stable, right now, I continued, and return his property from the safe.

And I'd give him a hundred dollars to make up for the terrible injustice.

Messenger smiled for the first time since I'd met him. Maybe for the first time in his life.

"This *surely* makes up for it," he said.

Almost, I said, and locked the front door with my spare key after we left.

Carmody spent the next day burying bodies and fixing up the office.

I helped.

No one had claimed the bodies of any of the Demkos. I didn't even know which were Demkos and who were unrelated hangers-on. Only two of them had any identification and their last names were not Demko and there was no way to trace next of kin or anything like that.

I put the property in the safe. There were several Bibles and pictures and the like. I can never get over how many criminals carry Bibles, but I'm not one to judge and I can't bring myself to throw away Bibles or pictures of girls or children; they meant something to somebody, once. I have a pretty big pile.

The dead men had carried a collective total of sixty-one dollars and some change. I put it in the safe, too. We'd spend it for ammunition and office supplies and such. I kept pretty close track of official money and didn't comingle it with my personal salary, even though there was no one to check on my accounting and no way to do it.

It had been an expensive week for me, what with my donations to Harbold and Messenger. That was my money, not the town's. But I do all right from bounties and rewards, so I wouldn't have to live on beans until my next paycheck.

Most of the guns I kept and locked them up in the cabinet, except for three that were cobbled-together junk. I took them apart and smashed the barrels with a hammer.

I let Carmody bury Salona. She had some jewelry and a little money and I gave it to Jaffe before he and the remainder of the troupe left town.

After lunch, Carmody put a new pane of glass in our office window. I held it while he fussed worked on it.

I always managed to hold it the wrong way, to hear him tell it, as he fussed with the corners while he fit it in.

Then he fixed the hole he had blasted and repaired some other sections of wood the termites had digested, and I have to admit he did an excellent job. Carmody measured and sawed and fitted new planks like a master carpenter.

I held pieces of wood and drove an occasional nail and listened to him scold me about how I didn't know how to hold wood or drive nails.

I complimented Carmody on how he could finish all these repairs so speedily.

"It ain't really about working fast," he said, somewhat absently. "It's more a matter of having the whole project laid out in your head. You get all the stuff in one place right from the get-go and think ahead about how you'll use the tools and materials."

That made sense, I agreed.

"Kinda like how you plan it all out how you intend to use people in your schemes," he added.

I didn't reply. I knew what was coming and nothing I said would change the thrust of the upcoming lecture.

"When we left the theater during the fracas you told me not to show my face and not let them see I was tall. You actually had this whole crazy scheme worked out in your head right after you figured out that Lefler and Gandolfsson would have known each other?"

"Not exactly," I said, which was true.

Carmody set down his carpenter's square – maybe the first and only such tool this town had ever seen — and regarded me with what I took to be genuine curiosity.

"When I saw Layton and thought he might be Lefler," I said, "I started thinking about my mission, and I started thinking like I was still on the mission. It just kicked in. And when you're in that pattern, you make a dozen plans in your head because you never know which one you might have to follow."

I took a second and collected my thoughts because I'd never actually, well, *collected my thoughts* before when it came to what I'd done in that brief interlude in 1864.

"You were a dead ringer for Gandolfsson," I said, "except for the hair and you being so short."

He raised an eyebrow. Probably no one had ever called him short and I was happy to break that new ground.

"Did I have it in my head right at that moment," I said, "that I'd get you to put on a wig, put lifts in your shoes, and talk with a Swedish accent to rattle Lefler so I could confirm his identity? No. If I'd hatched a plot like that full-blown it would have seemed ridiculous and far-fetched. When I did begin to think it through, it still seemed sort of implausible, but everything fell into place."

"Meaning what?"

"Meaning we had access to an actor who knew makeup and, presumably, could do accents and teach you how to talk like a Swede. And, of course, we had *you*, who not only looks the part but has a flair for impersonations. I heard Elmira cackling the other day when you two were stocking the bar and talking about how hard it was raining and I stood outside and got wet and listened."

I stuck my chin in the air and planted my hands on my hips and did my best imitation of Carmody imitating me.

"And did I ever enlighten you, my dear, about where that phrase 'raining cats and dogs' came from?" It's from back in the middle ages when animals would try to get warm by climbing on thatched roofs but when it would rain heavily – are you still with me my dear? – they would be *washed off the roof*. Are you still following? Isn't that brilliant? *Am I not brilliant*?"

"I don't remember saying that last part," Carmody mumbled, and then he cleared his throat and picked up a hammer.

"Anyway, I said, it turned out to be not such a crazy idea. Maybe it *was* a crazy idea – but it was so crazy that I don't think Lefler would have ever dreamed we'd cook something like that up. And you, my friend, were superb."

Carmody thanked me.

It came out *thank yee*.

And then he started pounding again, harder than before, grateful to change the subject, I think.

We finished at about seven. The last chore was to move the safe back against the newly mended wall. Carmody slid the safe a couple inches but one of the feet caught in the space between two floor planks.

He stopped and stood straight, took a breath, and wiped his sleeve across his forehead. Even Carmody gets tired. For him, that was like a normal man clutching his chest and dropping to the floor.

I set my armload of tools down and walked over.

"Don't need no help," Carmody said. "Just going to catch my breath."

I picked the safe up, a good two feet off the ground, and carried it to the wall, where I let it drop harder than I had to.

For emphasis.

And then we left and I took a long, hot bath before going to the Spoon.

My back hurt like hell.

I played piano pretty much straight through the evening. There was only one fight and I broke that up, as Carmody put it, with alacrity and a left hook.

It turned out to be a long, liquid evening.

I again congratulated Carmody on his acting ability, and he said it wasn't the first time he'd trod the boards.

No kidding. He said 'trod the boards.'

The kiss at the end was a stroke of genius, I told him.

"I figured Lefler would get it," Carmody said. "He done that preaching bit during the show and all. He must have known his scripture."

Elmira was puzzled. She goes to church – the church she built, on the other side of the bar and bordello she runs – but doesn't get much involved with the details.

"Judas betrayed Jesus and identified Jesus to the soldiers by kissing him," Carmody said.

"Nice touch," Elmira said, and poured herself another whiskey.

Carmody declined to sing *Silver Threads Among the Gold*, even though we'd forgotten to return the sheet music when we wheeled the piano back to the saloon and all the words were written out for him.

"Don't need no song to remind me 'my cheeks are growing hollow and life is fading fast away,'" he said, and then I remembered that he'd heard the song during the show and probably remembered all the words, anyway. His mind works that way.

"Sure as hell don't," Elmira said, thickly. When she gets drunk she doesn't show it much except that her lips don't move quite right.

"Cheer up," I said. I noticed my lips weren't working that well, either. "Some good came out of all this. I closed a chapter in my life."

"When you buried her?" Elmira said.

She regretted it as soon as it came out, and even with her leaden lips she managed to say she was sorry in the same breath.

"Carmody buried her," I said, "and that's not what I meant. I meant that I got Lefler – and closed that chapter. I didn't kill him, but he'll be buried long before he's dead. Harbold will find a nice Mexican jail where Lefler will never see daylight again."

I wanted to say one more thing, as I usually do after my fifth whiskey.

"When President Johnson — "

"Proud Tennessean," Carmody said, and took a drink.

"Yes, when the President from Tennessee ended prosecution for war crimes, he said that we couldn't keep fighting the war forever. I guess he was right. But that doesn't mean we have to *forget*. We can't forget because then it'll happen again. It'll always be on the horizon."

Elmira and Carmody stared straight ahead.

I believe they were thinking about things they would like to forget, but can't.

"There are always two horizons in your view," I said. "People don't think about that, or don't think about it enough, anyway. There's one in front and one in back. Unless you clean up things in the past, the horizon in back of you, the far horizon is just going to be more of the same."

Elmira wanted to change the subject.

"Will Harbold get in trouble?" she asked.

"In the impossible scenario that any of this comes to light," I said, "all he has to do is say that he followed my directions and picked up a short man in a buckskin jacket. If anyone's at fault, it's me. But how was I to know that Lefler would steal Messenger's coat?"

"But you knew?" Elmira asked.

"Of course I knew," I said. "People like him don't change."

"How about people like *you?*" Elmira said, and she began to cry.

It was unexpected but I had a pretty good idea what had brought her crying jag on.

"She meant nothing to me," I said, and it was true. "It was during a war and I was on assignment and she used me and I used her. Those were different days."

Elmira looked down at her clasped hands.

I knew what the real problem was. Elmira was no hothouse flower. She'd seen violence and death in abundance, but always grew cold and distant to me after she'd seen the aftermath of death that had been at my hands.

And now she'd seen another round of it and been confronted with the revelation that I'd been an assassin.

"It was another time," I said.

"I'm not Josiah Hatch anymore."

She got the reference to my alias, and she wiped her nose on her sleeve with a snorting sound I'd more readily expect from Carmody, and then she fashioned a weak smile.

"Josiah Hatch is dead," Carmody said suddenly, poking that absurd finger in the air. I noticed that he'd stopped pouring shots and was drinking straight from the bottle, his third bottle of the evening, I think, and was pretty well cucumbered, as he tended to put it.

So I played a few bars of a funeral dirge.

Everybody looked at me, of course, and Elmira got embarrassed, as usual, and waggled her fingers at me, laughing even though she didn't intend to. So I switched to an up-tempo jig.

"Josiah Hatch is dead," Carmody said, raising his glass.

"Taking the eternal dirt nap," I added, doing the same while I played left-handed.

Elmira poured herself another shot.

"And the war's over," she said, raising it in a toast.

"It's over," Carmody said.

"Yes, the war's over," I lied, and changed tunes again.

THE END

About the Author

Carl Dane is a career journalist and author who has written more than 20 nonfiction books, hundreds of articles, and a produced play. He's worked as a television anchor and talk show host, newspaper columnist, and journalism professor.

He was born in San Antonio, Texas, and has maintained a lifelong interest in the Old West and the Civil War. He is a member of The Sons of Union Veterans and has traced many of ancestors not only to the Civil War, but also to the War of 1812 and the American Revolution.

Carl often writes and lectures about ethical dilemmas, and has a deep interest in morality, including questions of whether the ends justify the means and how far a reasonable person can go in committing an ostensibly wrong act to achieve a "greater good."

He has testified on ethical issues before the U.S. Congress and has appeared on a wide variety of television programs, including Fox News' *The O'Reilly Factor*, *ABC News World News Now*, *CBS Capitol Voices*, and CNN's *Outlook*.

Carl is also interested in the structure of effective and eloquent communication, and has written two recent books on professional writing and speaking for a commercial academic and reference publisher.

Reviewers have consistently praised his work for its deft humor.

When not coyly writing about himself in the third person, Carl lives in suburban New Jersey, where he is active in local government and volunteer organizations. He is the father of two sons.

The characters of Josiah Hawke and Tom Carmody – and the situations they confront – were drawn from the author's interest in the darker sides of the human soul, and the contradictions built into the psyche of every man and woman.

Hawke is an intellectual, a former professor of philosophy, who became drawn to the thrill of violence after the life-changing events of the Civil War – which not only exposed Hawke to violence but showed him that he possessed considerable untapped skill in that area. Carmody, yin to Hawke's yang, is a blunt backwoodsman who is no stranger to violence, either, but has fought for survival and not for sport. Carmody wonders if Hawke's philosophical justifications are merely a smokescreen for seeking out trouble – and he's not afraid to tell that to Hawke.

Follow Carl at www.carldane.com

Made in the USA
San Bernardino, CA
13 September 2019